Al
Schnupp

CATLETT, VA

ZERO
Copyright © 2021 Al Schnupp

ISBN: 978-1-7348324-4-0

First paperback edition published by Cabal Books
May 2021

www.cabalbooks.us

Book Design by Michael Kazepis

Cabal Books
DBA Thicke & Vaney Books
P. O. Box 223
Catlett, VA 20119

THE CALL

Zero was rusting on the sofa, eating triple-fried pork rinds and watching two whackers thump one another on the Dazzle Box. His wife, Maxie, sat nearby, upright, in a leopard-print holster chair. Her knitting needles were clacking furiously as she applied a fresh row of knots to the bewhiskered scarf.

When the Dazzle Box switched into commercial drive, Maxie spoke up, "Zero, it's time to get off your bottom cheeks!"

"What's gnawing at your nag bone now?" growled Zero.

"Life is clipping along, and what do you have to show for yourself? Nothing! Soon you'll be rotting in the boneyard. Without a single accomplishment to your name."

"My god, woman," Zero snapped, "I drive a Muck Truck for Pa. And Pa is one of the richest men in the orb."

Maxie grunted. "Your Pa's a putz."

"Don't besmirch Pa. Whenever there's a festival, Pa is paid lots of dings and dongs to set up his platoon of privies."

Maxie stopped knitting. She looked over the roof of her spectacles. "Spare me!"

Zero shifted his gaze from the Dazzle Box to his wife. He smiled sparingly, revealing a set of stained yellow teeth. "Those privies are prize-winning. They are painted the prettiest shade of pink and smell as pleasant as a patch of posies."

Maxie sighed. "That's your highest ambition? To drive a Muck Truck and slurp up poo and piddle?"

"Frogs alive! Somebody has to do it. If it weren't for Pa and his privies we'd be penniless." He tore open a fresh bag of rinds.

"Every night you come home, smelling of muck. It's disgusting." She tugged on the ball of yarn and resumed her looping. "You could be so much more," she added.

"Phooey."

"With a little moxie," Maxie said, grinding her teeth, "You could be Icon of Groad."

Zero sank further into the cushions. "Me? Icon of the most pugnacious country in the orb?"

"Indeed!"

"Why would I want to do that?" snorted Zero. "I get to cavort with all the women I want here in Drudgeville."

"Death to Drudgeville," Maxie said, spitting out the words. "I hate Drudgeville. It's a mucky old town."

"Dilly wits! What's come over you?"

Maxie clutched the scarf. "I long for the flamboyance of Weaseldork."

Zero was unimpressed. "Weaseldork? The capital of Groad? There's nothing there but crimps and criminals."

She twisted the ball of yarn with her aching fingers. "I wish to eat in top-knife restaurants, attend the opera, and resuscitate myself in luxurious spas."

"Why this sudden interest in Weaseldork?" asked Zero. "And what makes you think I want to be Icon? I'm not a politician."

"Who says the Icon of Groad must be a politician?"

"By chiggers, Maxie, you're right," Zero said, experiencing a hasty flash of heat in his groin. Suddenly the light in Zero's eyes dimmed. "But everybody loves our current Icon, Rodney Ricochet. Won't Rodney be running for another term?"

"No," Maxie chirped smugly. "Insider sources say Rodney is suffering from sideway spirals. He plans to retire from politics and move to the seashore to build sand castles."

Zero smacked his palms together.

"Imagine," Maxie whispered, the needles digging into her thighs. "Millions of people, from every ripple of Groad, going to the polls, drawing the curtains shut and pushing your button, Zero."

"God, that's titillating. It invigorates my bully bag."

"Envision it," Maxie hissed, as she swayed in the chair. "There you are, on election night, on the Dazzle Box, everybody shouting, 'Zero! Zero! Zero!'"

"My god, woman, you know how to wiggle my weasel."

She was breathless. "Picture the inauguration. Everybody in the entire orb, erectus, moved to tears, as you're sworn in."

Zero resisted. "Maxie, what makes you think I could shimmy to such heights? Who put this percolator in your gizzard?"

"One of the most gallant men ever to have lived. A true genius. Horace Hickborne."

"Who's he?" asked Zero.

"Perhaps if you read the Ink Splotch, you'd know. Horace Hickborne is Chairman of the *Ratchet Party.*"

Zero exhaled. "You are quite the scheming hen, Maxie. Always pecking behind my back."

Maxie laid the scarf across her knee and stroked it lightly. "Horace and I . . . have become very accustomed. He's convinced you could become the next Icon. In fact, he agreed to manage your campaign."

Zero lifted his drink. "Maxie, I'm not a gas bag. My intelligence quota is minuscule. We have no credits or envies. I'm Zero!" He drained his glass of sugar-shined water.

Maxie swallowed and spoke in her sweetest possible voice. "Your Pa has a glut of riches. If he gave you his surplus, Horace says he could jumpstart the campaign."

"Pa won't part with his holdings." He poured himself another serving of the frothy brew.

"True. The man is a hoard hound. But you're his only heir, poised to inherit his trove of goodies upon his death."

"Forget it," Zero advised, fluxing his tongue. "Pa plans to live a very long time."

"Perhaps fate has other plans," suggested Maxie. "Perhaps your Pa was meant . . . all along . . . to have a short life."

"I beg your pardon?"

She continued, "And it is up to us . . . to see that fate is carried out."

Zero choked. "Maxie, are you nursing some nasty plot to do in the old man?"

The knitting needles were fluttering at top speed. "Zero, I'm flabbergasted! Where did you ever get such an idea? I had no idea you entertain such grisly thoughts."

After employing his skullbox for a few moments, Zero shifted forward in the sofa. "I have the perfect solution! A way to snuff the crackerjack without ever getting caught. In no time at all, Pa's fortune will be ours!"

"Then you'll do it?" Maxie gasped. "You'll run for Icon?" Her joints were crackling with delight.

He struggled to rise from his perch. "Who can stop me? I'm Zero!"

"So, what's your plan?" she inquired?

Pulling up his trousers, Zero began pacing the room. "All the poo and piddle we slurp from the privies is dumped into a huge vat. The muck generates a foul, noxious gas. I'll simply fill a bottle with those toxic fumes."

"Excellent!"

"When Pa is asleep we'll sneak into his bedchamber, uncork the bottle and park it under his nose. Within minutes, the old fart will die of asphyxiation."

"What a glucose idea!" exclaimed Maxie.

"We'll be rich! And nobody will be the wiser. The noxious gas will vanish—without a trace." Zero raised his head and uncorked a luxurious burp.

Maxie clapped her hands together. "Jubilee! Sometimes the spritz that escapades from your blowhole is so juicy!"

He rubbed his belly. "I do have my geyser moments!"

Maxie laid the scarf aside and jumped to her feet. "It's going to happen! I feel it in my serger. You *will* be Icon of Groad!" She wrapped her arms around Zero's expanding waist.

"Pa may curse me for killing him, but surely he'll forgive me when I become Icon and reconstitute his name." He tugged on his lobes. "When do I get to meet Mr. Hickborne?"

"As fate would have it, he's here!"

"Here! In our very own hovel?"

"Yes! Drinking a spider grog on the veranda." She called his name, "Mr. Hickborne!"

Horace swung aside the shuttered door and entered the den. He wore a tailored suit with broad grey and lavender stripes, paired with a stiff shirt, checkered vest and red bowtie. His cheeks were as ripe as tomatoes and he sported two silver-plated teeth. His slick, sculpted hair was combed over his right eye. The Chairman refused to stop smiling. "Allow me to introduce myself! Horace Hickborne, Doctor of Phraseology, Chairman of the *Ratchet Party*."

"The pleasure is mine," Zero announced.

Maxie was beaming.

Zero stepped forward. "You overheard our conversation?"

Horace waved his hand. "Don't worry. Your secrets are safe with me. Aren't they, Maxie?"

Maxie concurred. "Horace is the most prudent man I know. You can depend on him. He is enthralled with you, Zero. He'll always keep your best interests in mind."

"By the time we move into Icon Mansion, I will know everything about you, Zero," predicted Horace. "So, please, consider me part of the cluster circle."

"Oh, we do," volunteered Maxie, jiggling her jugs.

Horace encircled Zero, examining him from his tangled strands to his swollen toes, "Look at you, Zero. The very profile of an Icon. Honestly, Zero, you fit the role magnificently! Of course, we can all use a little makeover. We'll do something with the hair. Pull it out, perchance, and replace it with a toupee. Perhaps alter the chin. Rearrange teeth. Give you spectacles. Change the wardrobe. But, enough!" He brushed the empty bags of rinds off the coffee table, stepped on it, and struck an authentic pose. "First things first. Zero, it's time to snuff your old man!"

THE SNUFF

The trio of high-steppers hadn't counted on the fact that Kipper, Pa Zero's beloved dog, slept with him. At a young age Kipper lost both his hind legs when Step-Ma Zero hurled a bowling ball at the pup for spying through the mail slot and barking viciously at the handsome letter carrier, who Step-Ma Zero was glossing for a noogle.

From that day forward, Pa Zero only contorted with his second wife using one of three slurs: "Hell not no!" "Bugger off!" and the stinger—from a play he once heard—"You mangled, fly-bitten, pox-marked barnacle!"

Unable to troll about, Pa Zero had a miniature Muck Truck manufactured for Kipper. It was fitted with a harness. Strapped in, Kipper could once again race around the house, avoiding Step-Ma Zero and slathering Pa Zero with unbridled affection and slurpy kisses. Step-Ma died in a most suspect fashion—collapsing after receiving a manicure, her nails painted in a dazzling shade of crimson polish.

Maxie, with prying eyes and a curious kidney, had memorized the code to unlock Pa Zero's front door. A suspicious Kipper stared up at the trio. After a disapproving scrutiny of the imposters, Kipper turned, jogged down the hall—claws clacking, wheels rumbling—and scurried up the ramp to Pa Zero's bed.

"Oh, dearie," Maxie muttered. "I am not one of his favorite toys."

They listened for the unbroken duet of Pa Zero's onerous intake and outward wheeze, then tiptoed across the living room, into the hallway.

"I'm levitated Kipper didn't get snarky with you," Maxie whispered to Horace. "He rarely orchestrates with strangers."

As they walked down the hallway, Kipper began growling. A low, throat-song of unresolved menace.

"That mutt's gargle will wake up Pa!" cried Zero.

"Perhaps we could lure the bugger into the kitchen with a goose steak, then lock him in the pantry?" offered Maxie.

"Does the beast like tuna?" asked Horace, rummaging through the refrigerator.

They heard the sound of Kipper strolling down the hall.

"If we took the wheels off his Muck Truck," Zero said, "he'd be unable to vehicle. We could sneak into Pa Zero's bed without Kipper stalking us."

Kipper poked his head around the door frame, peering into the kitchen.

Horace held up a strip of bacon. "Here, boy. Nice boy."

Kipper's eyes narrowed. He took a step back and hacked up his dinner: a soup of soft, undigested venison curds.

Zero opened the front door, then returned to the kitchen and knelt on the floor, eye level with Kipper. "Can't you go outside? I just want to be Icon of Groad."

"Kipper!" It was Pa Zero, calling from the bedroom. The chihuahua spun around and scurried to his master's side.

Horace closed the refrigerator door, leaving the intruders in darkness. They waited for Pa Zero to resume snoring.

Maxie suggested Zero hide in the hallway closet. She and Horace would once again lure Kipper into the kitchen. Then, Zero could creep down the hall, close Pa Zero's bedroom door and carry out the asphyxiation. When they turned on the kitchen light, Kipper was there, standing by the stove, studying them, having overheard the entire conversation.

"How did you get here?" asked Horace.

Kipper replied with a low, unpolished growl. He trotted back to Pa Zero's bedroom and planted himself in the doorway.

"I have an idea," volunteered Maxie. "If we can't tease Kipper to do our bidding, we'll scare him. Spook him so hard, he'll racketeer out of the house, screeching, his tail between the wheels of his Muck Truck."

"How do we do that?" implored Zero.

"All of Step-Ma Zero's particles are stored in the subhouse," explained Maxie. "Let's go down there, find her trove of dresses and each put one on."

"I'd never slip into one of Step-Ma's dresses," Zero said. "Not with my manly measures."

"Zero, prop open the door to the garden, the street, the pool, the side porch, the storm shelter, the root cellar, the wine bin." She turned to Horace. "I think you'll look perfectly frightful in one of Step-Ma Zero's dresses."

The sound of someone ratting about in the subhouse was too much for the snoop dog Kipper. As Kipper stood at the top of the stairs, deciding if his Muck Truck could negotiate the steps, Zero snuck by him and closed the door to Pa Zero's bedroom. It would be impossible for Kipper to alert the old man.

The sight and scent of two Step-Ma Zeros climbing the stairs was too much for Kipper. He did a backflip, half twist and rocketed out the front door, into the street, under the carriage of a passing garbage truck and across the neighbor's lawn, leaving a trail of fright juice.

The trio waited outside of Pa Zero's bedroom door, listening. Certain the geezer was witless, they tiptoed inside and completed their mission.

THE TRIBUTE

Zero, stuffed in an under-size suit, stood next to Maxie and Horace as they surveyed the corpse.

"Your Pa never looked so good," Maxie declared.

"We've the mortician to thank for that," explained Horace. "He cut off his ugly facets."

Maxie ran her hand along the edge of the casket. "Horace, I hope this is a cheap dead-box."

"It is."

"There's no sense in spending good dings and dongs on a fizzled man," reasoned Maxie, "when it could be lavished on the living."

"My sentiments, as well!" confirmed Horace. "The dead-box is laminated cardboard. Bottom of the line!"

"Smashing!" Maxie cooed.

Horace patted Zero on the shoulder. "The down-taker did a nice job of fluffing his head fur."

Zero, still suffering from bouts of lightheaded guilt, remained skittish. "Are you sure the old sot is fully defrosted?"

Maxie socked her husband in the ribs. "Hush! He won't resurrect and crucify us with the truth." She whispered, "Zero, did the mortician pry the gold from your Pa's teeth as I requested?"

Horace extended his hand to Maxie. "Here, dear. As requested." He dropped several nuggets into her hand.

Tucking the tooth-fillers in her handkerchief, Maxie announced, "I'll go stash them in the lock-box." She slipped through the drapes that framed the enshrined cadaver.

With Maxie gone, Horace didn't waste any time sharing his concern. "Don't tell Maxie, Zero, but our attorney, when he read your Pa's will, discovered he bequeathed his fortune to Arnie Brewster."

"Arnie Brewster?" repeated Zero. "Who the screwhead is he?"

"No idea," admitted Horace, "but our attorney, Mr. Bucket, is investigating the riddle."

Zero was flustered. "You mean some undeserving stranger is destined to get all Pa's dings and dongs?"

"It's only a minor setback."

Horace's words failed to console Zero. Fearing he was about to be swindled of his inheritance, Zero addressed his pickled father. "You demonic louse!" He hit the old man, a solid thump on the chest. "I'm your son, your only offspring, you turnaround coat; the rightful heir! I need those dings and dongs if I'm to become Icon of Groad!"

"Don't worry," appealed Horace. "Mr. Bucket is a top-niche attorney, fully versed in debauchery. You'll get all your desserts."

Zero gave the corpse a second thump—a hard whack in the jaw. A plug of cotton catapulted from the dead man's mouth. His dentures fell, clacking against the lower, hollow teeth that were stripped of their metal. One eye jumped forward, out of its socket.

"Muzzle yourself!" Horace cried.

"How will I acquire my assets?" inquired Zero.

"Mr. Bucket will destroy your Papa's will and replace it with one he wrote." surmised Horace. "You'll get your rightful Zero allocation."

Zero wiped the sweat from his jowls and sidled up to Horace, "I'm counting on it."

"Now help put this old vessel back together," Horace ordered, ramming the cotton down the old man's throat.

Maxie returned, flushed and breathless. "Fireballs forever! Did you get a look at all those lurchers outside the funnel home?"

"As I predicted!" Horace gloated.

Zero peeked through the thick dark curtains. "There must be a thousand lurchers waiting to pay homage to my father."

Horace corrected him. "They're really here to see you, Zero."

Maxie was bewildered. "To see Zero? That doesn't make sense."

"Your mate is about to become the richest man in Groad, thereby guaranteeing he will become the next Icon," suggested Horace. "They wish to plaster him with their poohs and pahs."

"Oh, jelly," swooned Maxie.

Horace continued. "Just watch. Those lurchers will do anything to make an impression. They'll give Zero their best full-tooth smile, agree with everything he says, and shower his ears with chum plugs."

"Shall we let them in?" asked Zero.

"Indeed!" cried Horace. He cautiously instructed Zero, "Remember, be buddy bosoms to every lurcher. We need their endorsements if you wish to become Icon."

Maxie stuffed another set of air bags into her bra.

Horace danced about the parlor. "Let the boohooing begin."

Maxie raised her arms. "But where's the down-taker?"

Horace tipped his hat and bowed. "I gave him a bottle of plum hooch and said, 'Go whore yourself; I'll oversee the operation! Open the door, Zero! Maxie, look glum!"

From her purse, Maxie pulled a can of pungent spray. "Quick, Zero. Douse your eyes with tear juice!" She punched the nozzle and showered his face with the fiery liquid.

The first mourners admitted to the sanctuary were greeted with a touching scene: Zero writhing in pain on the floor, tears streaming from his swollen eyes.

"Did you ever see such love of a son for his father!" exclaimed someone.

Horace personally greeted each guest. "Thank you for coming, Mr. Updredge."

"I wouldn't miss it," cooed Mr. Updredge. "Such a tragic calamity!"

Horace turned and introduced the shifty-eyed mourner to Zero. "Mr. Updredge is publisher of *Groad Gazette*. Largest Ink Splotch in the country."

"I hope you fancied your father's obituary in *Groad Gazette*," offered Mr. Updredge. "We devoted a whole page to him."

Zero was uninterested. "Pa was a rat. I never gave him two shits to the wind."

"I despised the man, too," admitted Mr. Updredge.

Maxie joined the chorus of disapproval. "You were a doofus, Mr. Updredge, to waste paper on that imp."

"Well, Zero, if you ever need exposure," Mr. Updredge said, observing the crowd, "The *Groad Gazette* is at your service. My Ink Splotch is overlooked by millions of people."

"Rest assured," Zero promised. "You'll be hearing from me! I would love to have my pretty mug slathered all over *Groad Gazette*."

Horace tugged at the elbow of Zero. "This is Miss Greedo. Head of *Consolidated Energy*."

The stately woman was swathed in black. Although her suit was creaseless and she tittered in spotless lacquered shoes, her stockings had collected in folds at her frail ankles. Her face was obscured by a veil. "My sympathies, Zero. Such a tragic loss. Your Pa was a genius."

Zero cursed. "Blather tots! I hated the old fart!"

Miss Greedo found his remark highly amusing. Her shoulders, like pistons, pumped in time with her seesaw cackle. "Now that you mention it, I did find the conundrum dull."

"The man was a dreadful thumper," volunteered Maxie. "I hated his shank."

Miss Greedo reached under her veil and adjusted her tracheotomy valve. "Zero, your father purchased all his petrol from me. I hope, if you continue the privy business, you'll collude with *Consolidated Energy*."

"Of course, he will," promised Maxie.

Miss Greedo stared at the impertinent speaker. "Who's this?" she asked Zero.

"My wife, Maxie," explained Zero.

Miss Greedo was uninspired. "Oh." She did a slow eyeroll while appearing to clean the chandelier dangling above the casket with her lashes.

Maxie clutched the hand of Miss Greedo. "Tingled to meet you," she uttered.

Miss Greedo withdrew her hand, nearly losing her glove in the process. She pinched Zero slyly on the cheek. "Keep the contracts coming, Zero. Don't disappoint me."

Suddenly Horace bellowed. "Dolphie! You old fiddle stick!"

Blank-eyed Zero shrugged his shoulders.

"Dolphie is Chief Promoter of *Sputnik Transportation*," explained Horace. "Biggest manufacturer of automobiles in the orb."

Dolphie, endowed with oversized teeth, leaned forward. "Allow me to unload my condolences, Zero. Your father will be missed. I supplied him with a fleet of powerful Muck Trucks to pull around his privies."

"And fine mechanicals they were," Maxie said, nodding.

Horace was bubbling with enthusiasm. "How's Eureka?"

"We've divorced!"

"Ducky for you!" Horace said enthusiastically. "That side saddle was sopping cargo."

Dolphie ran his tongue across his teeth. "Zero, you look spiffy. The tonnage around your midriff is very becoming!"

"Well, compliments to you, too," Zero said, returning the praise.

Dolphie grinned lustfully. "Zero, I hope you and I can continue where your Pa and me left off."

Bypassing the line of lurchers, a couple snuck in a side door. The gentleman, lean, with a cautious air, wore an artist frock and beret. Even to the untrained eye, it was apparent he wore a false mustache. His partner, a tall leggy female, carried a smart briefcase that was trimmed with coarsely-stitched straps and metal studs. The couple was none other than the wily wizarding Inspector Oodles, private detective, mastermind of cheap disguises, and his assistant, Minnie.

The pair paused before the casket, looked at Pa Zero and then at each other. Then, as if to extract the last thoughts of the lifeless man, the artist placed his right hand on the face of the corpse.

Horace remained at his post, facilitating introductions. "This is Mrs. Stringent. She founded *GaggyMart*, the longest chain of parasite stores in Groad."

Mrs. Stringent was tightly wound. Her lifeless hair was dyed matte black and pulled back into a severely braided bun. A corset did its best to conceal several rolls of fat that hugged her ribs.

"Charmed," Zero said.

Mrs. Stringent was curious. "I'm so sorry about your Pa. What caused him to fizzle?"

Horace interrupted. "We haven't a clue. The flesh-hacker hasn't filed his report yet."

"We suspect he choked on his chortle," interjected Maxie.

"Well, the man was a huckster," announced Mrs. Stringent. "Wherever I built a *GaggyMart*, your Pa would set up his privies for the construction workers. They loved his crap shacks. Tarty girlie calendars. Bodacious holes in which to shit. Paper as fluffy as goose feathers."

"How many *GaggyMarts* have you built, Mrs. Stringent?" asked Horace.

"Three thousand, six hundred, fifty-seven. I won't stop until every town in Groad has one. Heavens," she said, pointing toward the artist. "What is that ghastly man doing?"

For the first time, Horace noticed the intruder. "I have no idea." He approached Inspector Oodles. "Excuse me. What are you doing?"

The gentleman feigned innocence. "Is there a problem? Do you smell a rotting plum?"

"Why are you rucking the corpse?" asked Horace. "Isn't that a bit creepy?"

"I won't be long," promised the artist.

Maxie was impatient. "Horace, have this corpse fondler thrown out and drubbed."

The imposter objected. "It is most comical that I finish my task."

Horace stepped forward. "I don't believe I ingested your name."

"Please. Silence," requested the artist, raising his hand and placing a finger over his mouth.

"He is consorting with the carcass," explained his female companion.

Horace raised his voice, "Who are you!"

The mysterious woman scolded Horace. "Lower your voice! The master of mirrors and smoke is trying to pulley up the last thoughts of the de-fizzed man."

But Horace had exhausted his patience. "I demand a litigation!"

The artist complied and introduced himself. "Pierre Entre. And my assistant, Mademoiselle Cardou."

"Please!" Horace muttered. "Skedaddle! Foreigners are not welcome here!"

Pierre Entre was not put off. "But I am obliged to create a sculpture of Monsieur Papa Zero."

"Nobody wishes to have a replica of the old man," retorted Horace.

The artist appeared dismayed. "I promised him."

"Pierre swore to petrify Monsieur Papa Zero's wishes," verified Mademoiselle Cardou.

"A sculpture? Of Pa?" smirked Zero.

Pierre stroked the face of Zero. "You are son of the defizzed. No? I cannot be mistaken. The resemblance is extraordinary. It could be you in the dead box!"

"You must be pranking!" cried Zero.

"I swear," insisted Pierre, "your Pa jingled me on the ringer."

Mademoiselle Cardou flashed her eyes. "I heard the entire conversation."

"'I wish to have a sculpture of my carriage,' your Papa said. 'It is an urgent matter,' he cried, 'The sculpture must be contrived immediately, for I sense I'm about to de-fizz!' His exact, precise, unpolluted words."

"Pierre gathered his carving tools and here we are!" reported Mademoisell Cardou. She opened the case. Inside were three telescoping pipes which she screwed to a sturdy wooden disc. On this tripod stand, she threw a large chunk of unformed clay.

Meanwhile, Monsieur Entre, fingering the face of Pa Zero, had grown deeply serious. "Your Papa had a premonition of his defizzacation. Why do you suppose that was?" he asked Zero.

Horace, whose chest was expanding to an alarming size, issued an order to the artist. "Remove your digits from the face of Pa Zero! I insist!"

"Listen," Pierre gasped. "Your Papa speaks without saucing his words! We slow-dance together. He whispers nuggets, little confidences, secrets of dark deeds in my ear. You cannot hear?"

Zero froze. "Really?"

Horace exploded. "This is hog wash! I shall have you thrown out!" He went to beseech several valets to help banish the imposters.

By now Zero had fallen under the spell of Monsieur Entre.

Dazed and confounded, Zero uttered, "My de-fizzed Pa will un-blossom his thoughts?"

"Naturally," he assured him. "All legumes by him will be spilled."

"Well, I'll be forked!" Zero clamored, his cornballs shaking in their pouch.

Mademoiselle Cardou laid her hand on Zero's shoulder. She waited for the scent of her perfume to overtake Zero. "Is possible your Papa may recall his final moments . . . and say how, as life was torqued from his body, he defizzed!"

Zero clutched his lower lip. "Egads!" he cried, biting down hard on his knuckles.

Pierre remained calm. "Go on! How did your Pa de-fizz? Ask him."

"Never!"

"Ah, you no wish to tango with Pa Zero's decrying flesh?" Pierre questioned. He took a moment to rethink his strategy. "We touch the clay, instead," he said diplomatically.

His assistant demonstrated. "Place your hands here. Like so. Press. It feel marvelous."

"Really?" Gingerly Zero reached out and tested the clay. "Like so?"

Cardou sighed. "Is not soufflé! *Both* hands. Press! Deeper! Harder! Like so."

Pierre egged him on. "Fondle it, the way you would fondilize the bosom of Mademoiselle."

Zero's face lit up. "Ooh. That twiddles my fancies!"

"Very good. Nice." Cardou added a long, languorous moan as Zero embraced the clay.

"Excellent. We finished," announced Pierre. "We go."

Monsieur Entre guardedly held the clay while his assistant unscrewed and collapsed the legs, which she returned to the case. "Ah reservoir," they said in unison as they rushed from the parlor, leaving everyone befuddled. They had barely cleared the door when Mr. Bucket rushed in, followed by Horace.

"Mr. Bucket!" exclaimed Maxie.

The lawyer was fuming, "Where are those shysters?"

"Gone!" cried Maxie.

Horace blinked hard. "You let them get away? Why?"

Zero was oblivious to their concern. "Mademoiselle was quite taken with me. Did you notice?"

"There's something's wormy about that couple," Horace declared.

"That Frenchman twirled his mustache in a most despicable way," sniffed Maxie.

Mr. Bucket began his interrogation. "What were they doing here?"

"The man's an imposter," Horace said, turning circles, beating the air with his fists.

"Should we hunt him down and have him de-brained?" asked Maxie.

Mr. Bucket withdrew a notepad from his vest. "Tell me what transpired."

"Do you think the shyster suspects the old sod was murdered?" Maxie whispered in Bucket's ear.

Horace continued to dog Zero, "You didn't blather anything, did you?

"Not at all! I simply petted his ball of clay," cried the offended Zero.

"What?!"

Maxie curled her lips. "You should have seen Zero. Like a sot. About to drift into ecstasy, he was, thinking he was fondling the titties of that loose French pastry."

"Oh, dear," sighed Mr. Bucket.

"What?" asked Horace.

The wheels in Mr. Bucket's skullbox were whirring. "Zero's finger art is now imprinted in that clay."

"What would he do with my finger art?" whimpered Zero.

"Who knows?" Mr. Bucket retorted. "Decode them. See if they match those in the crime scene. Use them as evidence in a court of law."

"Does this mean I can't become Icon?"

The attorney relaxed. "Never mind. I have some palm-slapping news. My negotiations in court were successful. After I slipped the judge a fistful of dongs he became agreeable."

Horace pumped his fist. "Excellent."

"Jubilee!" cried Maxie.

Mr. Bucket rested his hand on Zero's shoulder and whispered to him, out of earshot of Maxie. "The will of your Pa—as rewritten by me—stands." Bucket raised his voice for all to hear, "Zero will inherit the entire estate, knickknacks and all. Here is your first installment." Bucket offered his client a check, along with a stack of papers. "Also, the flesh-hacker's report and his final bon voyage."

The documents were intercepted by Maxie. She quoted from the coroner's report, "'De-fizzed from natural causes.' Blah, blah, blah. 'no indication of fecal play.'" She cast the report aside and recited a line from the will. "'I would like a lavish granite headstone in the shape of a privy with an external flame.' Right. Like that will happen!" She continued to read, "'The house and all its furnishings are transferred to my darling daughter-in-law, Maxie.'" She blew Mr. Bucket a kiss. "How sweet. I had no idea he fondled me."

"In Pa Zero's version," admitted the attorney, "he had other names for you."

"There is more than one will?" asked an alarmed Maxie.

"No. Only one," Bucket declared. "I misspeak."

"Of all these vouchers," Maxie declared, sniffing the check, "this is my favorite." She waved off the crowd of mourners. "Well, let's say goodbye to all these lurchers and throw the old geezer in the mud!" She adjusted her bra and roundly excused herself.

Horace waited until Maxie was out of earshot. "Any word on Arnie Brewster?"

Mr. Bucket expressed regret. "He remains a mystery."

Horace cringed. "I'm worried this Brewster fellow might sabotage our plans."

"Don't worry," Mr. Bucket said matter-of-factly, "all is clear for Zero to campaign full-steam for Icon of Groad. If Mr. Brewster materializes, I'll muffle him with cuffs."

Horace wrapped his arm around the attorney. "I like how you apply the law!"

THE ANNOUNCEMENT

Groad Memorial Plaza, in the heart of Weaseldork, was crowded with Dazzle Box reporters.

Buzz Wizzie, Chief Anchor for GOD, was applying a fresh coat of makeup. Deemed the most trustworthy broadcaster in Groad, Buzz was the phantom owner of GOD. He wore elevator shoes. A staunch undergarment cinched his waist while aggrandizing his sunken chest and failing biceps.

Field Correspondent for RAG, Fay Luicious, was conferring with her staff as they scanned the fact sheets. She was as thin and uncompromising as piano wire. She survived on a diet of shredded, julienned or chopped lettuce. Her left ear, grommeted with seventeen studs, was not allowed camera time.

EGO Political Analyst, Cho Wong, was being fitted with a new earpiece. The contraption was branded with the logo of *GaggyMart*. Trained as a cosmetologist, Miss Wong's second job was as a consultant to Dragettes. There was a rumor she also produced hygienic breathing videos for media addicts.

Technicians were everywhere, drinking reduced coffee. Personal Assistants supplied them with freshly-filled cups. Apprentices disposed the discarded containers.

Several minutes before noon, the reporters and their entourage began to get into position. Lights were switched on. The stars of Dazzle Box adjusted their microphones. Specialists conducted sound checks.

Buzz was the first to break into the airwaves. "We interrupt the bedlam to bring you this breaking story."

Fay followed closely behind. "I'm standing in front of Groad Memorial where, shortly, we expect a bumper announcement."

Cho continued the barrage. "Hours ago we received a dispatch. An important communiqué will be issued here."

"It's hard to speculate what the news might be," admitted Buzz.

Referring to her notes, Fay asked, "Is it possible Groad is under attack?"

Buzz added his own, dire forecast. "Might a salami hit the west coast?"

Cho joined the chorus. "The Prime Munster of Fromage was caught in a triple cream love triangle with the Feta Affairs Officer and Ambassador Manchego."

Buzz found it hard to maintain dryness. "This is absolute mayhem," he said, as the camera panned the plaza where a throng of onlookers had gathered, seeking autographs.

Fay would not be outdone in the use of hyper-hyperboles. "This is a media hullabaloo of the highest order."

"All major Dazzle Box stations are here," Cho observed, as she contemplated who she might suckle to advance her career.

Fay, without moving her mouth, observed in a cool, detached manner, "Reporters are being trampled into scotch."

From the edge of the crowd, two newcomers to the media pandemonium were flashing press passes and making their way toward the makeshift stage. Their disguises were grossly transparent. Minnie wore a tight-fitting pink dress with a low square neckline. Her hair was anchored to the left with a large hibiscus. A pair of non-prescription glasses gave her an air of false authority. She carried a cow horn. Inspector Oodles' thick, bushy eyebrows shaded his entire face. His cheeks were disfigured, plugged with wads of gauze.

He mumbled, "How do I look?"

"Magnificent," gushed Minnie.

"My eyebrow keeps falling off."

"Perhaps I didn't use enough gummy goo. And me?"

"You, my dear, are completely unrecognizable! Truly ravishing! Where's the blow pipe?"

"Right here. In my front hand."

"Aim for Zero's neck," he directed. "The effect will be immediate."

"I practiced all morning," she assured him. "My tracheotomy is good."

"Is the voice trap machine on?"

"Yes. It's running contiguously."

"When the truth serum hits Zero, he'll instantly start blathering." Oodles milked his gums, hoping to generate more saliva.

"I know. I saw how it worked on you."

"At last we'll get a confession!"

"Every word Zero utters will be clamped inside the voice trap."

"Our mission will be accomplished!"

Buzz peered dramatically into the camera, "I was just handed a note."

"There is movement on the stage," Fay informed her audience.

Cho purred softly into her microphone. "I believe we are ready to hurl."

"Oh, frack," exclaimed Inspector Oodles, "where's my press pass?"

"You're holding it, my chipmunk," whispered Minnie, folding a fresh stick of gum against her tongue. She spoke softly into the cow horn, confirming its workability, while coyly inspecting the Inspector, "Testicles One. Testicles Two. Testicles Three."

Horace Hickborne climbed the stairs to the stage. Moving deliberately, he smiled at the photographers before regally claiming the podium. He took another long moment to enjoy the scene. Only when the crowd began to grow restless, did he address them. He first recognized the members of the press. "Air-punchers, wave-netters, and sieve-cloggers, thank you for coming. It is an honor to introduce you to Zero, man of the upcoming hour." His voice carried the weight of a statesman about to rescue a dying country. "Although few people have heard of Zero, this miracle worker will purify the water with a plan that will revitalize Groad. Without a scissors he will catheterize the citizens of this beloved land. Give a big chunky cheerio for Zero!"

"Oh, my god!" cried Buzz, unaware his remarks were being broadcast.

"Who is that toddle top?!" Fay asked her crew.

With the help of a hydraulic crane, Zero was hoisted onstage. A patriotic song was blaring from the speakers, but the fire flares that were scheduled to accompany the scene failed to go off. To boot, the harness failed its one job. Zero was flipped upside down. Maxie, screaming, scurried on and unbuckled Zero from his harness. He fell to the floor and after a long bout of screaming, ratcheted himself up, waving to the crowd.

Zero waddled to the podium. He leaned into the screeching microphone. "Salutations!" he blurted.

"Who is that gander goose?" asked Cho.

Fay was flipping through a book of file photographs, hoping to identify all the characters in the unfolding saga. "His wife, I suspect," she said.

Zero cleared his throat and began timidly. "As you've heard from all angles, our country is in a state of shameful shambles. Its citizens are bamboozled. Members of the *Sickle Party* cannot interlude with congregants from the *Screwzer Party*. Dogs may become man's worst enemy. The cost of scum remover has skyrocketed. The weather has turned foul. Mealy bugs are propagating and war with Snart, the land of savagers, is breathing down the chimney flue."

As Zero progressed through his speech, he began stoking the fires. "But all that will change," he bellowed, "because I hereby announce my candidacy for Icon. Join me, friends. Together let's march to Weaseldork and seize Icon Mansion!"

The speech ended as abruptly as it began. Zero stepped aside and nodded.

Compelled to upcharge the atmosphere, Cho stated the obvious, followed by a volley of teasers, "You heard it here, folks. The orb is about to change. The air will be reconstituted. Political life will be forever decomposed."

Fay resorted to standard industry practice: a blast of rhetorical questions. "What do you think? Is this a credible bid for office? How much do you suppose that hambone weighs? Can our country be led by Zero? Will Groad gravitate to this newcomer and garb his message?"

Horace reappeared on stage, slapping Zero mightily on the back. "That was a splendid speech. Full of Zeroisms!"

"Zero! A few questions, if we might?" implored Buzz.

Cho shoved her boom microphone into Zero's face. "How are you qualified to be Icon?"

"If you kept abreast of the news," replied Zero, "you'd know I'm the richest man in Groad!"

Horace stepped forward, "Which means, of course, he has provisions to help the poor."

"Did you ever hold public office?" inquired Fay.

Horace responded, "Throughout his life, Zero served the public at the pubic level. Next!"

"Have you heard Lili Loath, candidate for the *Sickle Party*, raised millions and millions of dongs?" asked Cho. "The soothsayers are predicting she will win in a slideland."

The bushy-browed imposter grabbed the cow horn from Minnie and spoke into it, broadcasting his question throughout the plaza. "Zero! Where were you the night your Pa de-fizzed?"

Zero bristled. "You bugger plugger. I'm gonna torque your tongue!"

Once again, Horace came to the rescue. "Zero was plucking his wife, Maxie, when the old man de-fizzed. She can a-testify to that."

"Zero, are you affiliated with any party?" called out Fay.

Zero cracked his knuckles. "Yeah. The party that has the most loopy juice and loosely jointed ladies."

Horace smiled tersely. "The man is a joker," he elaborated, "which I think we all agree is an essential quality for Icon-hood. Actually, Zero will be the official candidate of the *Ratchet Party.*"

Oodles was not about to be ignored. "There's rumor your Pa was murdered. Any comment, Zero?"

Zero kicked the side of the podium. "I declare!"

"The old geezer died from natural decay," testified Horace. "If you don't believe us, quarantine the flesh-hacker's report."

"If that juicer don't be-sleeve his questions," Zero uttered to Horace, "I'll have him de-brained!"

"What's your platform?" shouted Cho.

Zero turned to his advisor, a blank expression on his face. "I wear flat-footed, honest-to-ground shoes," he said.

Horace fielded the question. "Zero is for stuffing everyone's bacon with turkey."

Together, Horace and Maxie threw out a list of promises. "Zero will lock up the boogeyman."

"He will abolish headaches."

"He'll outlaw tornadoes."

"Forbid the sale of measles."

"Mandate prosperity."

"Under his leadership, it will be the era of Zero truth, Zero justice, Zero compassion and equality!"

"Join the revolution!" cried Maxie, hoping to rally the crowd.

"Now!" whispered Inspector Oodles. "Blow the dart!"

"Let's turn this country around!" implored Horace. "Make Groad great again!"

"Vote Zero. Get what you deserve!" bellowed Maxie. "Ouch!" She slapped the side of her neck. "What the hellfire was that?" She continued to swat her neck. The dart dislodged and fell to the floor.

"Did I hit him?" asked Minnie. "Was my sniper-hood good?"

"No! You arrowed his wife," replied Oodles.

Horace saw Maxie's eyes begin to glaze over. He turned to the reporters. "Thank you, harpies. We must exonerate ourselves." He struggled to hook Maxie's elbow so he might pull her offstage, avoiding further contact with the press.

Maxie, who was immediately unplugged by the truth serum, pushed Horace aside and grabbed the microphone. "I know Zero is my husband," wheezed Maxie, "and I know I promised to coddle him until death do we un-join but sometimes the man is a shit."

"What?" exclaimed Horace.

Stung my Maxie's admission, Zero was momentarily speechless. "I beg your pardon?!"

"Really," Maxie said, "He can be such a yapping fool."

Horace apologized. "She's teasing, of course."

"And don't you think the whale should shed a few pounds?" asked Maxie.

"This is what we in the politician racket, call a duplicity stunt," explained Horace. "Pay her no heed."

Maxie pointed to Horace. "Now, Horace, on the other hand . . ." Before she could complete her thought, Horace cupped his hand over her mouth.

"She jests," he said, dragging her offstage. "We'll put some sugar in her and get her sweet levels back to normal in no time."

"Inspector Oodles, what now?" asked Minnie. "Shall we hood-cap Maxie? Perhaps *she* knows if Zero de-fizzed his Pa!"

The Inspector adjusted his brows. "Excellent idea, Minnie. Clearly, the truth is surging out of Maxie's vessels. We will obtain Zero's confession from her."

The stricken Maxie had been escorted into the janitor's closet of a public restroom, where she was recovering from the attack. Oodles and Minnie fought their way through the crowd, pushing aside reporters, determined to interrogate their subject.

The investigating couple was met by Zero at the bathroom door, "Wait a minute," Zero growled, "where do you think you're going?"

"We simply wish to gibber with your wife. A moment ago, on stage, she seemed quite smitten with perpendicular pains. Please. We only wish to be assured that nothing is wrong."

Zero gave the couple a once over. "You look familiar."

"As members of the press we frequently appear on the Dazzle Box," Minnie said. "I'm sure you've seen us there."

"No," Zero said, scanning his skullbox, "I refuse to watch the Dazzle Box unless they're showing a whacking competition or girlie strut show." He jackhammered Oodles on the chest. "Sure as dumplings, I've seen you before!"

More and more reporters began to congregate around the restroom as Zero sized up the detective.

"I'm told I look like hundreds of people who resemble me," Inspector Oodles said.

Zero grabbed the jaw of Oodles. "I don't like your muzzle," he said, squeezing his cheeks. Both wads of stuffing popped from Oodles mouth.

"Oh, my god!" Minnie cried. "You dislodged his egg nodes!" She turned to the crowd. "Summon the police!" Stoutly, Minnie struck Zero with her purse. "You assaulted a member of the press. Shame on you!"

Zero ducked, shielding himself from her attack. "Leave it to beaver! Don't pummel me." He wagged his finger at the impertinent Mr. Oodles. "Not another word about my Pa!" he warned.

Hearing the fracas escalate to dangerous Richter scale decibels, Horace emerged from the janitor's closet. "Everyone, clear the area immediately! Fuse alert! A bomb in the vicinity. Onward. Rappel! Report of a ticking bomb! Ticking bomb! Ticking bomb!" When he caught sight of Zero fleeing, he tackled him from behind. "Not you, Zero!"

"But we'll be blown to nuggets!" Zero gasped.

"It's a hoax!" Horace explained.

"A hoax?" Zero echoed. "I thought they are extinct."

"I fabricated a lie to clear the area. We were in serious trouble."

"Fang diddle," Zero wheezed.

Horace described the scene. "Your wife is back there in the closet. Tied-up. With a shoe in her mouth!"

"Why did she do that?" asked Zero.

"Not her! Me! I tied her up!"

"Why?"

"Someone struck Maxie with a dart and infused her with truth serum," Horace replied. "She was yammering away, non-stop, talking about everything from her fancies to her furies."

"She didn't say anything foul or filthy about me?"

"This is serious business. We need to hire bodyguards and distribute sling shots." Horace pulled a zapper from his back pocket. "Here. My nasty rod to buzzer stick anyone who gets too close."

"Thank you. How does it work?" Zero placed the prod against his forehead and pulled the trigger. The device delivered a powerful shock that knocked him to the ground. "Sassafras! Jigger up the snout." Blindly, he stumbled to his feet. "My thongue ith numb."

Horace dusted off Zero's coat. "Nonsense."

"No. Weally. I can't thalk."

"You're fine," lectured Horace. "You just blew a gasket. Momentarily."

The dazed Zero staggered about like a drunken ox. "I'm thelling you, my thonge is thiwithed up in a thight knot, like a thlug. A thollen thlug."

"Tonight's the fundraiser," Horace reminded Zero. "Will you be able to talk?"

"I don't thwink I can."

"Shake around your tongue. Chew on it. Bite down."

"I can't thew. My jaw is thruck."

Horace raised his voice. "You have to be able to talk!"

"I'm thorry."

"Damn! Let's get you to a doctor."

"I dispithe dothers!" pined Zero.
"Who gives a torque! I'm not going to cancel that fundraiser!"

THE FUNDRAISER

The ballroom of the Swanky Hotel in Weaseldork was chosen as the site for the fundraiser.

Maxie, who'd recovered remarkably from her encounter with truth, was delirious. She had anticipated this evening for months and wore a dress made specifically for the event. The fabulous designer, Marcus Marko, had discovered a floral fabric in an upholstery shop that he claimed was absolutely perfect for his client. The resulting gown was a floor length affair with huge crimped roses, made from complimentary fabric, stitched on each breast. On the back, at the waist, Mr. Marko attached an enormous nest manufactured from coiled willow reeds. He filled it with stuffed birds and hollow ostrich eggs. To Maxie's delight, Marko had insisted on crafting a perfume solely for her. She wore it liberally.

Maxie positioned herself at the grand entrance, prepared to greet each guest.

Mrs. Stringent, founder of *GaggyMart*, was the first to arrive. The clips above her temples, designed to purge the folds around her eyes, were not cleverly hidden in her hair today.

"Mrs. Stringent!" Maxie exclaimed. "Salutations. Welcome to Zero's Campaign Kickoff!"

The tycoon offered the hostess a frozen smile. "This is my husband, Floyd," she said. "He doesn't have anything to say. So I refuse to let him speak."

Maxie extended her hand. "So churned you could come!"

"I wouldn't miss it," Mrs. Stringent said honestly. "Your husband could be the next Icon of Groad. There are opportunities to be had." She poked her husband in the ribs. "Floyd! Don't stare at the staff!"

"How is business?"

"Superb. We opened three new *GaggyMarts* just this past week."

"Congratulations!"

Mrs. Stringent excused herself. She guided her husband to the bar. "Floyd, would your park yourself here while I go intercourse with interesting people?"

Maxie welcomed the publisher of *Groad Gazette*. "Mr. Updredge! How delicious to see you again." Freshly pigmented from a recent session at a tanning salon, Mr. Updredge glowed. He sported a new, pencil-thin moustache which was embellished with eyebrow liner.

"Hello, Maxie," he cooed. "Have you met Lucy, my mattress partner?"

"No," Maxie tittered. "Charmed to make your acquiescence, Lucy."

"You'll have to excuse her," Mr. Updredge explained in hushed tones, "she has perspiring sores on all three lips. It hurts to talk."

"Perhaps she could keep Floyd company," suggested Maxie. "He's also speaker-less."

"Truthfully, Maxie, we shouldn't be here," admitted Mr. Updredge.

"Why?!"

"I was ordered to appear in court."

"Oh, horrors!" exclaimed Maxie.

Updredge shrugged. "It's nothing. I'm always being shackled into court for publishing fallacious stories in *Groad Gazette.*"

"Talk to Horace," suggested Maxie. "Perhaps he can have the judge de-fizzed." She offered him a tray of hors d'oeuvres. "Help yourself to humdrums."

Maxie's proposition intrigued Updredge. "What a goose-bump idea!" he swooned. "De-fizz the judge! If he were found liverless in his bed . . . I'd be sure to repay Horace with a slug of pretty stories about your chubby!"

"I'll see what I can do." She directed her attention to Chief Promoter of *Sputnik Transportation.* "Hello, Dolphie!" For the affair, Dolphie had attired himself in a kilt, dashing jacket and woolen hose. Curtain tassels had been substituted for the flashes.

"Maxie! Don't you look riveting!" he exclaimed.

Maxie blushed. "As do you! I hope your dong holder is crammed with dongs . . . and you're in a generous mood."

"Perhaps we can negotiate something later." Dolphie presented his most recent, eleventh wife. "This is Fancy. Temporarily indisposed. Her jaw is wired shut."

Maxie gasped. "How unfortunate!"

"Not at all! She lost a hunch of pounds and the house is as quiet as a whistle."

"If only we could wire the jawbone of Zero together," confessed Maxie. "How is business at *Sputnik Transportation?*"

"A bit sluggish, I fear. The competition has taller, stronger crutches. I'm hoping Zero can do something about that if he becomes Icon."

"Oh, I'm sure he will, Dolphie." She caught sight of Miss Greedo. "Gwendolyn! Galloping embraces to you."

The Head of *Consolidated Energy* smiled broadly. "Maxie! Always a pandemic!"

"Who's the handsome sportster?" inquired Maxie.

"This is Hank. My day boy. Normally he locomotes at a lubricated level but today he has laryngitis."

Maxie clutched his hand. "Hello, Hank."

Miss Greedo interrupted, "Just imagine, Maxie, if Zero is elected Icon of Groad you will be First Female."

"I know! Isn't it gripping?" Maxie dabbed the drool from the corner of her mouth. "I'm absolutely flushed with grittiness. I trust things are going well at work?"

"Yes. *Consolidated Energy* continues to consolidate. We're unstoppable!" She hiked up her loose stockings.

"Keep us in mind when we pass the dong cup tonight." Maxie's attempt to enlarge small talk fell short.

"I need a drink," the humorless Miss Greedo said, re-waxing her lips. "Where's the faucet?"

"Next to the toiletries. Please. Go, chug some loopy juice. We have bottles and bottles of the stuff."

Dolphie reappeared and extended his hand to Miss Greedo. "I understand you're low on frizzle. Come, chug a drink with me while I ogle the waitress."

Miss Greedo accepted.

Horace joined Maxie. "How's it going?"

"Having the time of my life," gushed Maxie. She adjusted her waistband, which had a tendency to ride up, causing the sides of her skirt to flair even further over her hips. "It's hard to tell if the gang is in a grumpy or generous mood."

Horace assured her, "I've heard nothing but good reports."

Maxie spun around. "Could you check my bun bow nest? It's not out of alignment, is it?"

"It's flawless," Horace said.

Maxie beamed.

"I predict a banger night," ventured Horace.

As excitement mounted, Maxie continued to orchestrate the arrival of guests while Horace waltzed among the crowd, showering compliments on the most powerful citizens of Groad. When the attendants were sufficiently laced with loopy juice, Horace claimed his position at the head table. "Everyone, we're about ready to begin. Please take your seats. We have prepared a big evening. For the sake of extra-spousal intercourse we ask that husbands and wives do not settle next to one another."

Maxie had her own set of directives. "This is a jug-filled event. Bibs are located under the seat. Should you require barf bags, they are stowed in your gift basket. The silverware, which has been engraved with Zero's autograph, is complimentary. Please don't caress the flowers as some are highly sentimental."

Horace raised the pitch of his voice. "Are we all settled and feeling flawed?"

The crowd cheered.

Maxie announced the agenda. "After a brief address by my husband Zero, Deedeedo, star of the silver screen, will swish us with a few musical contortions. This will be followed by a seventeen-course meal, free-lance dancing, ruckus games, and unrestrained incantations."

"So, Ladies and Groin-diggers," thundered Horace, "without further fare-fan, it rouses my joy button to present the man we honor tonight: Zero!"

The beam of a spotlight swept over the audience and landed on Groad flag. Zero, who'd been secluded in a side room all evening, burst through the paper banner to great applause. He was not about to cut their drunken reception short. "Don't let me stop you. I love hand-thrashing." After Zero had wrung the last possible kernel of acknowledgment from his audience, he spoke. "Well, isn't this a peachy glory group of rich old snugly chums! Grapes to you! And many happy thumps for coming tonight. Hold on one second. I'd like to unloop my belt a prick or two. There we are. Perhaps it would also be a good idea to upsize my trousers." He paused to re-gird himself. "Begging your condolences! Well, as you know, I just announced my candidacy for Icon and, tonight, we beseech your assistance . . . to help mobilize the masses so the few, like us, can reap the side wind of their downfall. What say you, Ladies and Groin-diggers? Will you suckle me? Will you float the campaign so we can sink our tubers even deeper into the concrete? Hail. Hearty!

Ho! Thank you!" He initiated another round of applause and sat next to Maxie.

Horace provided the follow-up. "Ho! Ho! As Zero implicated, we beseech your assistance. Any contribution will be soundly rewarded. The payback will be stupendous. When Zero converses Icon Mansion he will fumigate the Outhouse and enact blunderfull laws that will reward each and every contortionist here. All it takes is a few dings and dongs."

Dolphie wanted specifics. "Will you impose a tariff on all foreign automobiles?"

Horace responded without missing a beat, as if the moment had been scripted. "Indeed, Dolphie! If Zero is elected, the citizens of Groad will find it fiscally prudent to buy your autos and *only* your autos."

The crowd cheered.

Mr. Updredge, owner of *Groad Gazette*, stated his aspiration. "Can you slap a lawsuit on *The Post*, *The Tribune*, and *The Herald*? Prohibit them from publishing?"

"After clipping the laws," Horace assured the publisher, "*Groad Gazette* will be the sole newspaper in the entire country!"

The crowd cheered even louder.

Miss Greedo stood. She directed her question to Dolphie. "Would you support a program to re-engineer your automobiles so they gullet twice as much fuel as they do now?"

Dolphie flashed his enormous teeth. "I don't see any problem with such a plan."

Having won the approval of the businessman, Miss Greedo now sought political approval. "Think you can manage that, Zero?"

"Consider it done," replied Horace.

"Yes. Consider it done," Zero said.

Again, the crowd cheered and the Head of *Consolidated Energy* smugly reseated herself.

Mrs. Stringent wished to have her interests addressed, as well. "Will you require every town to build a *GaggyMart*?"

"Sounds like an excellent, charitable program for the poor!" Horace said. "Of course, Mrs. Stringent."

"Well, groin-diggers, I'm impaled," Mrs. Stringent said. "You have my vote."

"Your vote, yes, of course," acknowledged Horace. "And, I hope, a few dings and dongs."

"How many dings and dongs do you want?" asked Miss Greedo.

"The more the merrier!" answered Horace.

Maxie explained. "We need dirt diggers, manure spreaders, nutcrackers, bumper thumpers, and air drops."

"Don't be shy," urged Horace.

"Give generously now and I promise to fill your coffins later," said Zero.

"Well, the *Ratchet Party* and its boys have my support!" Dolphie said.

Updredge followed, "Count me in!"

"To whom do we write the check?" asked Miss Stringent.

"To *Zero Investment*," directed Horace.

"Be sure to include lots of zeros!" cracked Zero.

The crowd roared.

"Is it time for our entertainment?" asked Maxie. "As promised, the glockenspiel Deedeedo has consorted to swag us with a few musical locomotives. Deedeedoo, come on out!" After a moment of silence, Maxie called, "Deedeedo, are you back there?" Maxie removed shreds of the paper flag to make way for the diva. "Deedeedo?"

A pair of entertainers emerged from the frame which held the demolished flag. The couple appeared to come directly from the slopes of Austria. The lad carried an accordion and wore lederhosen. His cheeks were bright red and he wore a badly-cut blond wig. His lassie sported two bouncing pigtails and an Alpine outfit. A tuba was perched on her shoulder.

The leader apologized. "We are so very sorry. Deedeedo has been dolloped with diphtheria."

"Deedeedo says not to worry. She a quicker bouncer backer from these attacks."

"We are here to take her place," announced Inspector Oodles.

"I will yodel while Fritz accompanies me on the squeeze piano," explained Minnie.

Maxie protested. "But I just saw Deedeedo an hour ago. She was curling her voice."

"It was an unusual case of diphtheria. Very powerful. Quick—like blitz bomb," the inspector said

"Will she be alright?" asked Maxie.

"Ja, ja."

"She was discarded to the sick house. Now, we perform."

The change of plans didn't throttle Zero. "I love yodels," he said.

Minnie removed the tuba. "Perhaps, Zero, you would be so kind as to provide the oomp to our pah pah?"

Zero jumped up. "Of course. What do you want me to do?"

"Why, play the tuba," instructed Oodles, "And set the beat for her yodels."

Zero frowned. "But I never trucked a tuba."

"Is easy," Minnie assured him. Just blow into the lip cup and tap the middle bobber.

Zero slipped into the instrument to the delight of everyone. He was about to blow into the horn when Mr. Bucket catapulted out of his chair and screamed, "DON'T TOUCH THAT TUBA!" The crazed attorney bolted forward and leapt over the table. He grabbed Zero with one hand and cupped the mouthpiece with the other.

Inspector Oodles and Minnie took refuge behind the loopy juice dispensary.

"But I want to toot my horn!" cried Zero.

"What do we do now?" Minnie asked Oodles.

"Remain calm," he whispered.

Zero threatened to disarm Mr. Bucket. "Release the tuba, or I'll buzz you with my shock rod!"

"The lip cup may be poisoned," Bucket insisted. "The moment you touch it, you'll de-fizz."

Minnie nervously tugged on her hair tails. "What if they discover the snake inside?"

"Don't fritter, my liebchen," the inspector replied. "The snake is very crafty. It will only emerge when the horn vibrates."

Mr. Bucket reached inside his coat. "Before you polka I must inspect the instrument," he said, wiping the nozzle with his handkerchief.

Oodles remained optimistic. "It will all come off as planned. The snake will hibernate until Zero plays the tuba, then it will slink out and bite him on the lip."

"Of course, we will deny knowing anything about the reptile," chuckled Minnie.

"We swear uppsie and downsie we never knew snakes are known to habitually sleep in tubas."

"And even though the snake isn't poisonous, we say it is."

"Precisely," chuckled Oodles. "That way, thinking he is about to de-fizz, Zero will confess his crime."

"Oh, Inspector," cried Minnie, "you are vicious! Finally Zero will spill his jelly beans."

Horace wanted the festivities to resume. He was pumping Mr. Bucket for information. "Are you suggesting these entertainers are imposters, scheming to harm Zero?"

"Who knows?" Mr. Bucket snapped the instrument with his index finger and listened intently. "I'm just being cautious."

"What's the uphold?" called out Mrs. Stringent.

"Can we get on with the show?" yelled Updredge.

Mr. Bucket determined the tuba was harmless and handed it off to Zero. "Go on. Have your toot."

"You want me to shock it with my buzzer stick?" asked Zero, "to detoxify any germs?"

"Halt!" cried Inspector Oodles, returning from his post.

"What now?!"

"A shock to the tuba," Oodles muttered, "would tarnish the metal, ja? And see how beautifully it reflects your cherub face? We wouldn't want to deglaze your angelic features. No shock! Shock bad!"

"No, no, we wouldn't want that," agreed Zero.

"Are we ready to play music then?" asked Minnie.

"Spiel!" commanded Oodles. He struck and held a simple chord as Zero teased a low growl from the tuba. Just as the two notes began to harmonize, Mrs. Stringent let out a horrific scream.

"Gott in himmel. What now?!" sighed Oodles.

Mrs. Stringent harpooned her husband. "Floyd you deceitful slug! Trading smooches with Fancy!"

Dolphie skewered his wife, "Fancy, you faithless toad! Sharing tongue with Floyd!"

Mrs. Stringent and Dolphie advanced on their cheating spouses. Mrs. Stringent removed a pin from her hat, intending to stab Floyd in the eye. Dolphie turned his cigarette lighter on high and fired the flint, preparing to torch Fancy's hair.

Floyd and Fancy scrambled behind Zero for cover as Mrs. Stringent and Dolphie advanced, weapons in hand.

"Don't prick me!" Zero cried, dropping the tuba. "Please don't ignite me! I'm allergic to pain!" The tuba rolled off stage, into the audience.

Mrs. Stringent missed Floyd's eye and delivered a jab to his ego, deflating his libido. Dolphie brutally singed Fancy's wild hair of infidelity.

The skirmish was interrupted with a roof-piercing scream. "Oh, my god," Miss Greedo screeched. "There's a snake on the loose!"

Oodles grabbed Minnie's arm. "My liebchen. Quick. Hide!" They dove under a table as Floyd and Fancy initiated the evacuation. Within minutes the ballroom was cleared of patrons. Only Horace, Maxie and Zero remained.

"Thank god they didn't reclaim their checks before they scrambled," Maxie said.

Horace was itching to tally the numbers. "Let me have a look." He flipped through notes, glancing at the figures. "This is quite a haul!"

Zero was peevish. "I never got to play the tuba," he reminded them, then added, "Did those performers look familiar to anyone?"

Maxie ignored his question. "We never got to eat. Deedeedo was a no-show. We didn't get to dance or dine. But, all-in-all, it went quite well."

Horace disagreed. "Zero was a disgrace. We need to lacquer his image."

"A disgrace?"

Horace accused Zero of gross gesticulation. "During the speech you flogged your arms about like a torpedo. You exhumed noxious fumes and your far side eye twittered."

"You're an old quagmire!" Zero snorted. "What the noodle do you know!"

"Horace is right," said Maxie.

Zero snorted. "I thought the speech was brilliant!"

"Hell not!" Horace replied. "Tomorrow we are taking you to the *Shimmer Clinic for Politicians*. The staff is marvelous. They perform amazing make-overs. They will inner-upside-down-out you."

"I don't like the sound of that," Zero whimpered as the three departed the room.

"The *Shimmer Clinic!*" Oodles exclaimed, emerging from under the table.

"You know of it?" asked Minnie.

"Ja! I will contact the *Clinic* and have them add my name to the list of their consultants."

"They'll be thrilled to hear from you, I'm sure." Minnie quivered. "You're the most famous nose-poker in the orb, Inspector Oodles."

Oodles shrugged. "Perhaps I overblow my reputation."

"I think we should just arrest Zero and lock him up," proposed Minnie.

"Don't leap to conclusions, my liebchen."

"We know Zero de-fizzed his Pa!"

"Nein. We suspect! We have inkling. But we cannot verify that fact. We need evidence. We need a confusion!"

Minnie fluttered her eyelids. "Oh, Inspector Oodles, you're right. We must take it slow. But couldn't a quicky pace—in some cases—be investigated?"

THE MAKEOVER

Shimmer Clinic operated out of a warehouse on the outskirts of Weaseldork. It was managed by Wanda Dupe, who advised numerous politicians and was, in fact, married to Senator Swipe, currently serving time in Stone Hedge Prison. Wanda was incapable of sitting down: the vertebrae in her spine had fused. Unfazed by her misfortune, Wanda navigated life with a rosy outlook. She laughed at cripples, rejoiced in the accidents of others, and tormented pets whenever possible.

Emerging from her office, Wanda heartily shook the hands of Horace, Maxie and Zero. "Welcome to *Shimmer Clinic*, where we transform lackluster politicians into sizzlers! I'm Wanda, the manager."

Horace presented Zero. "This is our subject."

Zero dug in his heels. "Transform, my shank! There is no need for any corrective gel. I'm perfection!"

"Zero, don't be a draggy foot," Maxie scowled. "We only want to gloss your image."

Wanda escorted the trio to her office. "I'd like you to meet our first consultant, Miss Groad."

Miss Groad, pale as a marshmallow, could not easily be mistaken. She had a sash across her chest that declared her title. "Hello, I'm Miss Groad," she said rather stiffly.

"Anyone who wishes to be Icon," explained Wanda, "must know his public. It would behoove you, therefore, Zero to commit a few statistics to memory. Learn some vital phrases. Study your demographics. They will serve you well."

Maxie nodded. "I've been saying that all along. Know thy pubic. Haven't I, Horace?"

"To facilitate your education," Wanda instructed, "Miss Groad, who represents the average citizen of Groad, will instruct us in the ways of Groadeism."

Miss Groad stepped forward. "Thank you. I'm Miss Groad because I embody Groadeism in every sense of the word. We have 14.3 guns in our house. Every Sunday we sashay to Steeple House and prostrate God. Before my 2.4 children could trombone the tricycle I taught them to pledge the flag of Groad. We have seven Dazzle Boxes which we watch seven hours a day seven days a week. I wash dishes with Jubilee. Hobstrap is our favorite food. At after past five we shop at *GaggyMart*. When our children get sick, I administer *Redux*. Everyday I apply a fresh coat of wishbone. Our son plays nail-ball which our daughter, who studies sidestepping, despises. We are six feet, ten inches in debt. My husband drives a buff cream auto. Next year I will divorce him."

Wanda cracked her knuckles. "Excellent, Miss Groad. She turned to Zero. "She is the bull's rump to whom you tail your message."

"That shouldn't be difficult," said Zero. He turned to Horace. "How do I do that?"

"Simple," Horace replied. "We glorify the value of guns, hold rallies in Steeple Houses, and plug the Dazzle Box with sugar pictures of you."

"Shall we move on?" Wanda herded the group out a side door, into a changing room. "Let's discuss apparel."

Miss Groad offered her analysis. "In Groad the typical choice of body cover is flesh clingers for girls. Knee knockers are popular with trundled couples. Men prefer pouch plungers. Upcycled paper fabric is standard among fogies over fifty. Although the citizens of Groad dress on the down side of taupe, they want their Icon to wear up garb. I'm Miss Groad."

Seth entered, pushing a manikin dressed in a gray suit. "This is our most popular version," he informed the group. "It is a nondescript, middle-of-the-gray spectrum, sateen suit, with snappy lapels, nappy pocket drops and obedient buttons."

"You want me to slip my curvaceous bacon in that locker-bag?" gasped Zero.

Seth concluded his oration. "The fabric also comes in dark, smoke or charcoal gray."

Zero was peeved. "Hell not, no!"

Wanda directed their attention to a second manikin; it displayed a gray suit, as well. "Perhaps this one is more appealing to your eye."

Seth clarified, "Our second option has a daring liner and six less counting threads. It is manufactured in Groad. The fabric is treated with slick-spray. Epithets will not stick to it."

"Excellent!" exclaimed Maxie. "Zero is often a target of rebuffs."

"This fabric also comes in dark, smoke or charcoal gray," added Wanda.

Zero rejected the outfit. "I'll never be able to execute myself in such a fiasco."

Seth rolled the dummy aside. "I understand. Don't trigger yourself." He presented a third manikin. It, too, was wrapped in a gray suit. "This is a more sporty, luscious design."

Wanda listed the features. "Notice the shoulders have been enhanced, exuding nobility of character. Most importantly, the material debars the penetration of bullets."

"We do expect attempts on the life of Zero. Several, in fact." admitted Horace.

Seth lauded its qualities. "The suit is treated with micro-glam. Notice how it glows. Isn't the effect mesmerizing?"

"Oh, Zero," Maxie cried, "this really would radiate your figure!"

"Anyone featured on Dazzle Box adores this suit," Wanda gushed. "It sparkles shamelessly under lights."

"We have seven Dazzle Boxes which we watch seven hours a day seven days a week. I'm Miss Groad." announced Miss Groad.

"The fabric also comes in dark, smoke or charcoal gray," concluded Seth.

"What do you think, Zero?" asked Maxie. "What will it be?"

Wanda described additional options, available for a modest fee. "Each suit can be ordered with a zipper-lock. Generally, the wife holds the key to the zipper-lock. The candidate cannot undo his trousers or unfurl his juice tube without her permission."

"I hate 'em!" Zero declared. "All of 'em!"

Wanda patted him gently on the back. "Whatever version you choose, we recommend a white shirt with a pink and green tie— the official colors of Groad."

"Pink and Green!" shouted Zero. "How cunning! The very colors of our flag!"

Wanda congratulated Zero. "Very clever. I see nothing escapes you."

Miss Groad snapped to life. "Before my 2.4 children could trombone the tricycle I taught them to pledge the flag of Groad. I'm Miss Groad."

"It's obvious?" declared Zero. "Shouldn't I have a pink and green *suit*!"

"Oh, Horace. I think Zero's on to something!" cried Maxie.

"It's brilliant!" Zero said. "I'm brilliant!"

Horace consented. "Why not! Be conspicuous, I say. Pink and green it is!"

"Let me place the order. We'll have it tailored within minutes," Wanda assured them. "In the meantime, why don't you meet our next consultant, the newest instructor here at *Shimmer Clinic?* His name is Igor! I think you'll find him grotesquely useful." She ushered the quartet into a dim storage unit.

Inspired by the promise of a dashing suit, Zero pawed at the arm of his manager. "Horace, I want to be on the Dazzle Box. Can I be on the Dazzle Box?"

"That's already in the works," Horace announced. "We plan to make our first commercial next week."

Igor was the brainchild of Inspector Oodles. Under his camouflaged outfit he wore a grossly overdeveloped muscle suit. His huge shoulders were severely out of proportion to his narrow hips. He had issued himself an eye patch and thundered about in platform shoes. Several scars had been applied to his face; tattoos adorned his neck. Minnie was costumed in a black leather corset, ringed with a belt of pelts. A black pageboy wig and charcoal lips contributed to her grim look. Oodles greeted his clients. "I Igor. This Zelda. We just finished our third breakfast—borscht."

"I was expecting something a little less . . . primitive," Horace whispered to Maxie.

Wanda took charge. "This is Zero, who wishes to be the next Icon of Groad. Please attend to his needs while I go obliterate a few chunks in the office."

Horace was reluctant. "What . . . kind of consulting do you do?"

Igor waved his hand dramatically. "We . . . perform magic acts!"

"Like sawing someone in half?" ventured Horace.

"It can be done!" Igor assured him.

Zelda was eager to join the conversation. "You tell us problem. We make it disappear."

Horace appeared only mildly interested. "Oh?"

"Whatever pricks your pretty," proposed Igor, "I poof!"

Horace nodded. "I see."

"Misbehaviors. Naughty gnats. Overhead bills. We make all go away."

"What gnats have you we should scrunch?" asked Zelda.

Maxie, still admiring the physique of Igor, adjusted her bosom. "My mushy heart. You muck away the nasties?"

"I crack neckbone of anyone. Just give me name." Igor seated himself on a crate of confetti.

"Did you hear that?" Maxie asked Horace.

Horace excused himself. "Thank you, Igor. I don't think we'll be needing your services."

Maxie resisted. "Not so fast, Horace. Remember that photographer? The one we discovered lurking in the closet after we did the knock-knock?"

"That sniveling weasel!" recalled Horace.

Igor fingered a scar on his chin. "It sounds like we have first our culprit." He nodded to Zelda, who held up a knife.

"What's his name?" she asked, ready to carve letters into her skin.

Maxie bit her lip. "I'm not suggesting you de-fizz him."

"But a woeful whooping would be nice," muttered Horace, "And dynamite all his photographs."

"What is name of him?" Zelda requested a second time.

Maxie shrugged. "I don't know."

"No need to fret," Igor replied. "We find closet man."

Zelda ran her finger along the edge of her knife. "Who else?"

"Everyone have long list of finks," admonished Igor.

"I have a cousin who skull-dashed me," admitted Zero. "I never repaid him for all his taunts."

Igor nodded sympathetically. "Relatives! The worst. I de-brain cousin for you."

Zelda winked. "It give Igor special joy to crack neckbone of relatives."

"I de-fizzed my own pa!" confessed Igor.

"I don't doubt it!" chuckled Maxie.

"Do you want me to de-fizz your pa, Zero?" asked Igor.

Maxie interrupted. "His pa is already de-fizzed."

The thug offered a knowing look and appealed to Zero. "How did he de-fizz? Who snorkeled him?"

Horace jumped in, snapping at Igor. "The man died of natural decay!"

But Igor persisted. "Perhaps a twisty uncle? Have you a naughty sister?"

"Zero is an only child!" cracked Maxie.

"How's your mum? Be she a sweet and goosey lady?" asked Igor.

Zero dropped his head. "One day she gummed wheels to her crutches and rode off. We never saw her again."

"I sorry. Me heart ache for your calamity. God bless your mum."

"Two days later Pa remarried. I never constituted Step-Ma; she was a nasty old coot."

Igor shifted. "I hope your Pa was a good femur to you. Tell me. Was your Pa a chum?"

"Enough about Pa Zero!!" shouted Horace.

"Not another word!" begged Zero.

"Where exactly are your headquarters, Igor?" asked Horace.

"We not from Groad," Zelda said. "Igor and Zelda from cold country. Near land of no sun."

Zelda, pretending to shiver, offered her hands to Igor who held them against his cheeks.

The group waited apprehensively. Would Igor make a meal of Zelda's hands or offer her a pair of gloves?

Igor rose. He swatted the light bulb and proceeded to walk along the edge of the room. "There are ways many to de-fizz a man, Zero. What, you think, is best method?"

Zero smiled. "I can think of several. One, in particular, is highly effective . . ."

"Zero, enough!" barked Horace.

"We have 14.3 guns in our house," announced Miss Groad.

Horace was getting edgy. "Where is Wanda!? Isn't that suit done?"

Igor stared intently at Zero. "I hear story perhaps your Pa had other children."

Horace nearly jumped out of his skin. "Preposterous!"

"Ludicrous!"

"The idea!"

"Impossible!"

"Who told you such a thing?" Maxie demanded fiercely.

"One never knows," Igor replied politely. "My Pa was father to thirty-seven munchkins. If any unexpected munchkin shows up, Zero, let me know. I poof them for you!"

Wanda burst into the room, brandishing the pink and green suit. "Here we are. Isn't it abhorrent? Go ahead, try on the coat." She introduced her tagalong helper, a miniature, very tan, eunuch. "This is Nester, our makeup consultant."

"Welcome to *Shimmer Clinic*, where we transform lackluster politicians into sizzlers!" Nester crooned.

Wanda smiled. "Will you be utilizing Igor?"

"His services are declined!" Horace said bitingly.

Wanda excused Igor and Zelda then guided the remaining group to the salon. Zero was seated in a large swivel chair before a bank of mirrors.

Nester took charge. "Voters adore politicians who have a smile that dazzles. Does our Zero have a dazzling smile? Or must we give his choppers a scrub?"

"I wash dishes with Jubilee," blurted Miss Groad.

Pulling back the lips of Zero, Nester surveyed the grinders. "A good scrubbing seems in order. I'll prescribe a strong abrasive." The consultant pulled on a few tufts of hair. "Who commands your straggly hair?"

Maxie couldn't restrain herself. "A queer barber from the mucky old town of Drudgeville."

"Clearly, it needs renovation. I suggest more grey on the gables. Researchers," Nester pointed out, "say an Icon should have fourteen percent cremated hair."

Maxie sat in the chair next to Zero. "Is there research on the coif of the First Female of Groad?"

"Yes. It should be stiffed and stuffed to the right. To keep the coif in its cubicle, spray it with haberdashery."

Maxie looked at herself in the mirror and saw Icon Mansion reflected in her eyes.

Nester resumed his examination of Zero. "Your cheeks are invalid. They lack color. Not good. Do you hoof-clog, even occasionally?"

"Chug my carcass on a spinner wheel?" asked Zero. "Lift iron spools? No, thanks! I have all the muscle I need without hoof-clogging."

"A little rouge, nevertheless," Nester said, "to give the impression of robustness."

"Everyday I apply a fresh coat of wishbone," spouted Miss Groad.

"Do you articulate when you get nervous?" Nester asked his subject.

"The man profuses like a waterfall," groaned Maxie.

"We'll shut down those drain pipes with an anti-varmint. An Icon should never, under any circumstances, articulate. I'll write a prescription. Do you wear aromas?"

"Oh, how I've begged him to douse himself with aromas!" Maxie cried. "To no avail. And he so needs it. . . ."

Nester selected a small vial from among his supplies. "This is a special aroma, Zero. A conglomeration of the glandular essence of six Iconers." He lifted the folds under Zero's jowls and gave them a light spray.

"Will it make the ladies swindle? Will they yearn to noogle me?" cooed Zero.

"They'll regale you all the way to Icon Mansion," Nester assured him.

"I do like the sound of that!"

The tray of aromas was set aside; it was replaced with an assortment of needles. "Now, I'm going to brand your forehead with invisible ink," explained Nester.

"A tattoo of sorts?" Zero surmised nervously.

"Exactly. Although no one will actually see the message, it will be perceived nonetheless. What would you like me to write?"

Zero looked to Nester for advice. "What do you suggest?"

"Most clients have 'trust me' branded on their skull," mused Nester.

Wanda suggested another oft-requested slogan. "'I'm human' is also popular."

"What about 'saint?'" asked Zero. "That'll noose 'em!"

"A good, honest choice," replied Wanda.

"Will this hurt?"

Nester strapped Zero into the chair and gleefully selected a size 9 needle. "If it becomes too painful, I'll give you a suppository," he promised.

Wanda cautioned Nester. "Be sure of the spelling. Remember out last client? Your error cost me a bundle."

"I know how to spell!" Nester countered, then mouthed the letters B—I—C—H—T—T .

Maxie had grown tired of Horace pacing the room. "What's wrong? It looks like you're about to blow a valve."

"It's preposterous!"

"What?"

"To think that Zero may have a brother or sisters. Did anyone ever mention this before?"

"It's the first I've heard of it," answered Maxie truthfully.

"Before my 2.4 children could trombone—"

"Would you shut up!" screamed Horace.

A half hour later Nester finished his work and boosted Zero into an upright position.

"You're looking quite transformed, Zero," remarked Wanda. "All polished and pruned, ready to make your first commercial for the Dazzle Box."

Zero clamored from the chair. "I'd like to have a good look at myself." He faced the mirrors.

Maxie sidled up beside him. "You certainly appear clashing."

"I rip quite a figure, don't I?" Zero announced, pulling the trousers over his pouch.

"What do you think, Horace? Go on. Tell Zero how he looks."

"I'm speechless."

"Oh," Maxie cried, "you can do better than that!"

"What do you want me to say?" Horace growled. "He looks like Zero! A big shiny, polished up Zero."

"Did you hear, Zero?" She blew Horace a kiss. "There now. That wasn't so difficult, was it? I'm in complete agreement. A big shiny, polished up Zero."

THE COMMERCIAL

Histrionics, a city just south of Weaseldork, was the entertainment capital of Groad. Numerous Dazzle Box stations, reel studios, and unfounded stages lined Starlet Boulevard, where *Air Unlimited* was located. After reviewing the claims of numerous companies, Horace had selected *Air Unlimited* to produce the commercials for Zero's campaign. The creative staff promised to craft a brilliant commercial that would make Zero a household name and surely propel him into Icon Mansion.

Crew members were making last-minute adjustments as Zero lounged by the buffet table, devouring everything in sight.

For the umpteenth time, Tinker checked the gauge on his camera. "When it reaches four hundred degrees," he announced, "we'll be ready to roll." Tinker, one of the best technicians in the business, had uncanny abilities. He could dismantle and reassemble a complex brass, spring-sprung clock in record time. It was possible for him to determine, within a few degrees, the number of lumens striking an object. But he couldn't tell anyone the color of the eyes of his best friend.

Zero turned to Edith, Head of Costuming. "I think they made my suit a size too small."

Edith brushed the sugar flakes from his jacket without uttering a word.

"Oh, Zero, it fit perfectly two weeks ago," sighed Maxie.

Devo, the acting coach, approached Zero. "Would you like to look over the script before we begin?"

"Bugger off!" Zero yelled, spraying the coach with a mouthful of cheese chunks. "I have it immortalized! What do you think I am? An idiot?"

Mild-mannered Devo, frequently and erroneously called Diva, was a valued coach to the stars. Desire and temperament, he maintained, were rooted in the heels of a character. Trigger the proper pressure point and personality would be revealed. When Devo examined the heel of Zero, he found it an indecipherable landscape of nothingness.

Through a small door in the corner of the enormous hanger stepped Oodles and Minnie. Slowly, like two marionettes, they shuffled towards the assembled crews. The pair resembled two deformed birds: an arthritic penguin and a narcoleptic stork. To disguise himself, Oodles had slipped into an inner tube and inflated it, then draped the whole affair in a fringe velvet housecoat. A monocle gleamed in the socket of his right eye. An ornate cane with a goose head was used to clear a path before him. Minnie had slipped into a pair of hip-hugger boots and a tent top. Her accessories included cat-eye glasses, enormous earrings, and a boa.

Oodles flexed his shoulders. "I hope I'm not late," he said, without moving his lips.

Strut, the director, glanced at the clock. "We already have an acting coach."

"Oh, no. I'm not a virtuoso of the stage. Although I could be."

"This is a closed set," Strut said brusquely.

"Apparently you didn't get the notice."

Minnie dropped her jaw until it appeared to unhinge. "We apologize."

Oodles explained their presence. "We hail from the Office of Oversight. Division Six. Department of Ethical Advertising Among Politicians. Think of us as watchdogs. Grrrrr."

"I never heard of such an organization," Strut said.

"Well, it exists whether you heard of it or not."

"Would you like to see identification?" asked Minnie.

Oodles continued, "Every commercial of a political nature must be shot under our supervision."

The camera operator interrupted. "Three hundred and seventy-five degrees."

"We won't get in the way," promised Minnie. "We simply wish to verify the accuracy of every statement."

"It is illegal for a candidate to blather false accusations. No exceptions," Oodles said, wagging his finger.

"Four hundred and fifty degrees."

"Misrepresentation . . . exaggeration . . . discoloration . . . in any form . . . will not be tolerated."

Mascara, the Makeup Artist, with the support of Horace and Maxie, began to quiz Zero. "Have you scrubbed your teeth?"

"Has your tongue been sanitized?"

"Have your ears been shoveled clean?"

"Has your nose been cleared of refuse?"

"Such a fuss!" Zero exclaimed, pushing them away.

"Five hundred degrees!" Tinker bellowed.

The director checked to see if everyone was at their station. "Are we ready?"

"How much acting do you want?" asked Zero.

"Zero!" Strut snapped. "Be yourself."

Zero registered his disappointment. "No acting? But if called upon, I'm quite the beefsteak."

"Six hundred degrees."

"No beef. No steak. No meat of any kind!" instructed Strut. "Just say the lines!"

"Okay. Okay."

"Seven hundred."

Zero planted himself in front of the set: a wall of framed portraits of the most inspiring, selfless heroes throughout Groad's history. Just out of camera range, the Properties Master rolled a life-size wax model of Zero into position. The lights were snapped on. As promised, Zero's suit glowed.

"Action!" cried Strut.

Zero began. "Hello, Zero. I'm Iconoclastic." He stopped. "I'm sorry. Can we start over?"

"Once more," directed Strut. "Action!"

"Hello, Icon. I'm Zero." Zero thumped the air with his fist. "My fault. Once more. I'll get it this time. I have it."

"Again. Action."

"Hello. I'm Zero, candidate for Icon." He began to walk toward the figure of himself. "'Who is this alien to politics,' you might ask, 'and what does Zero stand for?'" He placed an arm around the duplicate of himself. "I'm a chummy ah-shucks, ordinary . . ." The dummy fell.

"Cut!"

Zero kicked the uncooperative prop. "Why didn't I stay up?"

"Don't lean on the figure!" Strut muttered. "Just touch yourself."

"There's no need to yell!" Zero exclaimed.

Minnie, in her role of censor, interrupted. "'Alien,'" she mused. "Can he say that? Is that permitted? Isn't 'alien' a firecracker word in Groad, code for swamp critters?"

Mascara took advantage of the break to powder Zero's nose. "Just a quickie flambé, while they reset the scene."

"I suppose 'alien' is permissible," replied Oodles, flipping through a tattered manual. "It's not in the book of prohibition."

"Horace, where's that jug of loopy juice you keep in your back pocket?" inquired Zero. "I want a snorkel."

Horace handed the flask to Zero, who took a chug.

"Once again," announced Strut. "From 'Who is this alien?' Action."

Zero complied. "'Who is this alien to politics,' you might ask, 'and what does Zero stand for?'" He gingerly stroked the model. "I'm a chummy ah-shucks ordinary citizen of Groad who patronizes his country and longs for a shackleless future. Like you, I dream of a warm snuggly craggy-less bed."

Devo signaled to the director who yelled, "Cut!"

"Damn!"

The acting coach rolled his eyes. "The word is 'life.' A 'craggy-less life.' Not 'bed.'"

Zero pondered for a moment. "It just doesn't sound right, Diva. It don't come natural to me."

"I'm sorry. And it's Devo."

"'Bed' seems like absolutely, hoggishly the right word," argued Zero.

"We're not changing it," insisted Devo. "Stick to the script."

"Bed. You'd think I could remember that. Bed. Bed. Bed."

"No! 'Life!'" Devo screamed. "'Life!' And could you tone down the windmill thingamajig?"

Zero was taken aback. "You don't like the way I move my hands?"

The coach demonstrated. "One hand twist. Fine. A pointed finger or two. Okay. But this?" He thrashed his arms about wildly. "What is that?"

Zero stiffened. Slowly, he turned to Horace. "Did you hire this assjack?"

"He's the best director in the business," Horace said.

"I want him fired."

Maxie had it. "Zero, clap your trapper!" Her command was followed by a long moment of silence.

Finally Strut spoke up. "Take it from 'Like you, I dream . . .' Action."

Zero forged ahead. "Like you, I dream of a warm snuggly craggy-less life and feckless friends who share my orifices." He stopped and stared blankly into the camera. "Hello, I'm Zero."

"Cut!"

"I can't re-congeal the rest," confessed Zero.

Devo made a decision. "I'll write your lines on cue cards."

"Thank you. I could use the break. This is some damn hard work." He snatched two mayonnaise sandwiches from the buffet and offered one to the disguised Inspector. "What do you think? I think I'm doing one damn, heck of a good job!"

Oodles refused the sandwich. "We're not here to critique your acting . . . but . . . the way you walk. I must say. It's so like your father."

Zero backed up. "You knew my Pa?"

"We chummed on numerous occasions," Oodles proclaimed. "Watching you, Zero, is like Pa Zero is back from the dead. It's so spooky."

Horace saw Zero turn white. "Is everything dapper, Zero?"

Zero extended his finger towards Inspector Oodles. "This man says I look like Pa come back from the grave."

"Oh, dilly-dally," scoffed Horace. "You're under a great squeegee of stress. And . . . imagining things."

Strut clapped his hands. "Can we continue?"

"Horace," Zero whispered, "can you spare one more nip of loopy juice?"

"Zero, in this segment," gestured Strut, "While saying your line, walk to the table."

"Easy," Zero said, sneaking another swig from the flask.

"If we're ready, then, action!"

Reading from the card and walking stiffly, Zero marched toward the table. "If elected, I will lock up the boogeyman. Pick up gun."

"Cut. That's a stage direction. Pick the gun up."

"Huh?"

"From the table! Right in front of you. Again. Action."

Zero repeated the line. "If elected, I will lock up the boogeyman." As instructed, he picked up the gun. "Pick up gun."

"Cut! Cut! Cut!" cried Strut. "Don't say 'Pick up gun!' Just do it!"

"I understand! Don't pick up the gun. Just say it."

"No! Pick up the gun. But don't say you're picking it up!"

"Got it! Are we ready?"

"Go ahead."

Zero retraced his steps, speaking to himself, "Really? Like Pa Zero?"

"Go!" Strut screamed.

"I'm waiting for you to say 'Action!'" snorted Zero.

"Action!"

Zero cleared his throat. "If elected," he said, picking up the gun, "I will lock up the boogeyman." He squinted at the cue card, blinked, and resumed speaking. "The citizens of Groad will no longer experience fear." Cautiously, Zero replaced the gun and sat in an armchair next to the table. "If elected, I will sail a Groad flag . . ."

"Cut!"

Zero groaned. "What's wrong?"

Devo threw his arms in the air. "You said 'sail.'"

"Yes!"

Devo pointed to the cue card. "You're supposed to say 'send.'"

"'Send?'" Zero thought for a moment. "I said that. Strut, didn't I say 'send?'"

"I wasn't listening," Strut admitted. "Once more."

Oodles tapped his cane on the floor. "Why is he picking up a gun? Is he going to kill someone?"

Zero jumped out of the chair. "Who said that! Who said I killed someone?"

"Pay him no mind," pleaded Horace, handing Zero his flask.

"Maxie, get ready for your segment. Once again, Zero. Camera rolling."

Zero peered suspiciously at Inspector Oodles. "If elected, I will send a Groad flag to every hungry child in the country. I propose to manufacture more erasers and outlaw boorish behavior."

The camera continued to grind away as Maxie entered the frame to stand behind Zero. "Hello, I'm Maxie, Zero's wife. We've been cross-chained twenty-seven years. Although Zero and I haven't had any children, as First Female I'll change that. We consider it a vitality to populate the country of Groad with the finest possible livestock."

"Isn't she the shakes?" cooed Zero. "I will forever be in convalesce with her."

She smiled appealingly. "As one who excruciatingly knows the man, Zero is everything he purports to be. We all deserve the best, I say. We all deserve Zero. Vote Zero!"

"Cut," Strut sighed. "I think we have it."

Zero jumped up. "How was that? I was good, wasn't I?"

"Excellent!" Horace said, congratulating him.

"Was I sexy enough? Did I show my manhood? It's no stretch, is it, to think I could have a career on the stage?" Suddenly, the loopy juice sent Zero looping; he fell back into the chair.

"It was a stellar performance, old chops," Horace cracked. "You'll get the votes. No doubt about it."

Inspector Oodles cornered Zero, displaying his clipboard crammed with papers. "Just sign here," he instructed, "to verify that we observed the shooting."

"Shooting," Minnie repeated, laboring over the word. "Did I miss something? Was there gunfire? Has there been a murder? Is that the smell of sulfur?"

"Murder?" gasped Zero. He recoiled as Strut stepped in and snatched the clipboard.

"Oh, no. Not *your* signature, Strut," interjected Oodles. "I require the signature of Zero."

"I'd like to see that identification now, if you don't mind," Horace said.

Inspector Oodles bowed. "Happy to oblige you." He turned to Minnie, "The gentleman wishes to see evidence."

"Of course," Minnie said, shuffling through a folder of papers. With a deft flip of her hand, a photograph appeared to accidentally fall from the file.

"What's that?" asked Horace.

"It is of no interest to you, I'm sure," Minnie said.

Zero picked up the paper. "It's a photograph of Pa!"

Minnie leaned over Zero's shoulder. "Your Pa? Why would a photograph of him be here?"

"How did you get this?" Horace quizzed.

Inspector Oodles brushed off the incident. "I have no idea."

Horace picked up the gun used by Zero in the commercial. "I don't like the way this looks. Something isn't right. People don't walk around, carrying a picture of Zero's Pa in their briefcase. It isn't normal."

"You're going to shoot me?" Minnie asked calmly.

"It's a prop," said the Director. "There aren't any bullets in it."

Horace returned the harmless gun to the table. From inside his jacket he pulled a real pistol.

"Oh, Horace, don't!" cried Maxie. "You'll ruin everything!"

Horace laughed. "Just fooling ya. Having a tease. Why would I carry a real gun? This is one of those props guns, too. See for yourself." He threw the gun to the Camera Operator, who examined the weapon.

"It's a nice counterfeiter," Tinker declared. He pulled the trigger and the gun fired. The bullet crazed the concealed inner tube around the waist of Oodles. With a loud fizz, the tube began to deflate.

"Oh, my largesse," cried Maxie. "What have you done? The man is de-fizzing. Right before our eyes!"

"My tubes and my inners!" moaned Oodles as he grabbed the hand of Minnie. "Quick, get me to a mechanic."

Horace reached into his wallet and handed Tinker a fistful of dongs. "Thank you," he said. "Anytime you want to work for me . . . let me know."

"It was an accident," insisted Tinker. "Honest, Mr. Horace, an accident."

Horace slapped Tinker on the back. "An accident?" He winked. "Yeah, and when I wink, that's an accident, too."

THE SELECTION

Having retreated to Drudgeville, the hometown of Zero and Maxie, the trio reviewed their strategy. Their office was set up in the library. All the shelves had been cleared of comic books. In their place stood a collection of plates of various designs, free samples requested by Maxie from a host of manufacturers. From this assortment Maxie hoped to choose her Icon Mansion china pattern.

"It's time to choose your running mate, Zero," declared Horace.

"Someone to get pastries and courier my panties to the cleaners?!" asked Zero. "Thank you, Horace."

"No, someone to replace you in the event you die in office."

"Horace, you know I don't like that kind of talk!" scoffed Zero.

Maxie rolled her eyes. "Don't hyperextend your wet bone, Zero. You're going to live a very long life."

"That's what you said about Pa!" Zero whimpered.

Horace excused himself. A moment later he reappeared with a tall bearded man. They paused in the doorway, "This is Tad Ripper, Chairman of the *Ratchet Party*."

"At your service, Zero," Tad said, clearing his throat.

Zero studied Horace. "I thought *you* are Chairman of the *Ratchet Party*."

"I was," explained Horace. "I resigned. I'm your Campaign Manager now."

Zero exhaled painfully. "Someone ought to tell me these things."

"We know, sweetie; there's a lot to keep track of," Maxie said.

"Can we address the order of the day?" continued Horace. "The Committee for Vice Icon of Groad has sent over several candidates for inspection."

"Now?" exclaimed Zero. "I was hoping to take a vacation. To Sadie's Smorgasbord."

"I'm afraid that'll have to wait."

"All the contenders are outside," said Tad.

Zero slammed his empty plate on the breakfast tray. "Hell and humdrums!"

Maxie tried to calm him. "This won't take long. Afterwards we'll order in creamed ice."

Tad pulled up a chair and settled himself between Zero and Horace. He had a nose kinked enough to hang an umbrella on, if someone were so inclined. "Our first candidate is Lieutenant Berta Loone." Tad called for his secretary, Flo, who scurried about with aimless intention.

Flo presented the candidate, a lanky hardened female in full uniform. Her left hand was a reconstructed limb, fashioned from porcelain.

"Reporting for duty," she barked, clicking her heels and saluting.

"At ease, Berta," Tad instructed.

"But vigilant, Chairman Ripper. Always vigilant!"

Horace got down to business. "Berta, what makes you the plummy choice for Vice Icon?"

Lieutenant Loone liked his style. "Major Horace, I bring a frosty military backbone to your operation. Every war conducted by Groad has utilized my expertise as a soldier."

"That's very commendable," acknowledged Horace, "but Groad was defeated in all its military endeavors."

"Precisely, Sir, because our gunfire was too low," surmised the Lieutenant. "I hope to change that. Aim higher, I say!"

"My sentiments, as well!" Zero said. He drew Horace and Tad close to him and whispered into their ears. "I say we pick her and conclude these hearings."

Berta put a halt to their consultation. "If I might intercept any ingoing missiles."

"Fire away!" exclaimed Horace, chuckling at his own joke.

"Civilians!" the Lieutenant muttered under her breath. She resumed her role as commander. "Although my records indicate I sometimes over-bound my steps, you should know I was reprimanded only once by General Stutz, who has a shine for my medals."

"We're aware General Stutz cannot always control his torpedoes," Tad responded.

"Zero, I've been dutiful. I've done reconnaissance. One of your campaign slogans is to lock up the boogeyman. I affirm I'm the lady for the job!" Berta, certain her remarks had landed squarely on target, dug her heels into the slick, polished oak floor.

Tad was impressed. "Very good."

Berta wasn't finished. "Torture of the enemy—any enemy—internal or extraneous—is my specialty."

"Thank you, Lieutenant Loone," Tad said. "You may go."

Berta was shocked. "We have yet to discuss war plans!"

"It's on the agenda, Lieutenant," Horace said. "Bye."

After the Lieutenant stormed from the bunker, discharging bullets of discontent, Flo ushered in the second candidate.

Tad introduced the handsome mop-headed lad. "Here we have Pipe Dreams. He's fairly new to politics."

Pipe spoke with a disarming lilt. "I'm tickled to be considered." He had a voice that begged to be paired with a guitar.

"How would you be an asset to the ticket?" asked Horace.

Pipe hooked his thumbs through the loops of his jeans. "Like a dog who nips the trotter of a cow, I have the ability to corral people."

"We need someone who can herd the masses," admitted Horace.

Lieutenant Loone stuck her head in the door. "There are two firemen out here. They insist on coming in."

"Not now," Horace snapped. "We're busy. We'll sound an alarm if we need them."

It was the answer Lieutenant Loone wished to hear. "I'll order a blockade," she said.

Ignoring the threats of Lieutenant Loone, Inspector Oodles and Minnie burst into the library.

"How will you sound an alarm if the detectors of fire are disarmed?" inquired Oodles. The Inspector and Minnie wore matching anti-inflammatory uniforms. They each carried a toolbox and tempered claw axe. Oodles had attached a prosthetic knob to his nose and glued a set of buck teeth to his real ones.

Minnie, whose face was plastered with soot, spoke. "According to our schedule . . . we must inspect and re-surge each and every smokie detector and every fiery alarm."

Horace threw up his hands. "Well, be quiet about it!"

"Our apologies, Pipe," said Tad.

Oodles chuckled. "You won't even know we're here." He fondled a lamp as Minnie attached a listening device to it.

"So," continued Horace, "you can rope a steer. What else should we know about you?"

Pipe deepened his dimples. "People find me forthcoming. Just like a cow who spews milk when her twit is squeezed, I attract varmint to my bosom."

"I take it you were raised on a farm?" induced Tad.

"That I was. I like to think it a-testifies to my good nature. I'm of ordinary stock, as welcome as a weed in the garden."

Minnie inadvertently dropped the telephone.

Oodles cringed. "Sorry."

"Why are you futzing with the telephone!?" asked Horace.

"There isn't a smoke alarm in the innards of a phone!" cracked Maxie.

"But there should be!" said Oodles.

"That's why we're installing one," added Minnie.

Oodles quickly repositioned himself, blocking Minnie from view. She inserted an electronic ear into the carriage. Oodles explained, "Many a man, while flaring his pipe, has fallen asleep near the phone and caught fire."

Tad, wary of the fire-duet, closed his briefcase, which now contained a microphone in the disguise of a fountain pen which Minnie had slyly slipped into it. "Could we continue the interview?"

But Zero had other ideas. "I say we pick the farmer and conclude these hearings."

Horace proceeded. "Mr. Pipe Dreams, I have no doubt you can lasso the country pumpkin. What about city folks?"

Pipe inserted a plug of snuff. "My Pa used to say any pig will sup from a trough if it's primed with food. We just have to determine what city slickers like to eat and offer it to 'em. They'll come a-runnin'."

"Very good," replied Horace.

"If it's common sense you want, I'm the hand to hire," said Pipe. "Whatever the job—pitch a fork, peck a hen, hound a fox— I'll do it!"

"We'll let you know our decision as soon as we regurgitate the facts," promised Tad.

"Excuse me," Oodles said as he flicked the floor lamp switch several times.

"The lamp requires a detector?" asked Horace.

"Any combustible appliance," replied Oodles.

"Clear the decks!" Madge O'Malley wheeled herself into the library. "What kind of floor is this? No traction whatsoever. How am I supposed to get on? Something should be done about that. Oh, firemen! I like anything to do with a hose. What's up, boys?

That secretary out there. What's her name? Flo? She's a dorky dame!"

Tad smiled. "This is Madge O'Malley."

Madge cussed and said, "They know who I am!" The old woman, folded into her battered chair, wore a navy dress which didn't fully hide her tattered slip. Her thick, chunky black shoes and yellow bobby socks trimmed in lace made her spindly legs appear even thinner than they were.

"Hello, Madge," said Horace.

Madge clutched the arms of her chair. "Don't keep me waiting. Skip the taboos. You'll be wanting me as your Vice Icon, Zero, because, without my expertise, you don't stand a chance!"

"Miss O'Malley served in the Outhouse for sixty years!" Tad reminded everyone.

"Not a chance!" reiterated Madge, loading her voice with ballast.

Zero responded like a trained parrot. "I plan to fumigate the Outhouse if I'm elected Icon. Isn't that right, Horace?"

Madge nodded. "It does have a lot of cobs and webs! Have you got yourself a slogan, Zero?"

"We're working on it," Horace said.

"If you want to snag the fish, you need a catching tag-hook. That's how I see it!" Madge pushed back her glasses. "Hey! Fire-boys! Could one of you look at my chair. See if I have any spent spindles left."

"They're installing fire alarms," explained Maxie.

"Ah!"

Tad wished to question the candidate further. "Miss O'Malley . . ."

"Call me Madge!"

"There's concern, Madge," Tad said timidly, "given your age . . ."

Madge anticipated his question. "Oh, out with it, boy! Am I gonna croak on you? That's what you're asking."

Tad recalled, "You have had a few heart attacks."

"Those were love taps . . . priming the pumper for the next hundred years," insisted Madge. "Let's get cracking. Call our team 'The Zip of Zero. The Magic of Madge.' Everywhere. Banners. Blimps. Billboards. I got a printer in mind. Can you see it?"

Zero was growing impatient. "I say we pick Madge and conclude these hearings."

"What are you saying? Speak up, boy!" demanded Madge. "You have trumpet troubles? Me? I have the lungs of a lungfish. Just ask the men who served under me."

Horace unfolded his arms. "Is there a way to sit more upright in your chair?"

"You want me to throw out my titties?" asked Madge.

"Go stand beside Madge, Zero," instructed Horace.

Zero heaved himself from the exhausted chair and took a position beside Madge.

"I see," mused Tad.

Madge was clueless. "There's a problem?"

"As a couple, you look mismatched," observed Maxie.

"I'm old, for god's sake," snapped Madge. "Old people shrink."

"Perhaps a taller wheel chair," suggested Tad.

Horace concurred. "A high chair wheel chair!"

Madge wasn't amused. "Despite what you say! I got size! That's my thought."

Horace dismissed her, "Thank you, Madge. That'll be all."

"I'm telling you. I can still stir the soup." Madge spun around, popped a wheelie, and rolled out the room. The fishing pole, lashed to her chair, to which a flag was attached, snapped violently against the door frame.

With Flo outside, refueling herself with vapors, and nobody to introduce him, Sid Thomas presented himself before the committee. "Am I in the right place?"

Tad looked through his papers. "This is Sid Thomas." The candidate wore a ribbed turtleneck and a paisley corduroy jacket with leather elbow patches. It seemed his feet were welded into his shoes, which were fused to the floor.

"What should I do? Where should I stand?" asked Sid.

"Wherever you wish," replied Tad.

Sid didn't move. "Is this okay? Why am I here?"

Tad smiled. "The *Ratchet Party* thinks you're a prime candidate for Vice Icon."

"They do?"

Horace urged Sid on, "Tell us about yourself."

"What should I say?"

"Whatever you wish," said Horace.

"Is there anything in particular you're looking for?"

"No, but I like your tone."

"You do?"

"Very much," Horace confirmed.

Zero disagreed. "He's all wrong! I don't care a frigate for him. The man's a bully!"

"Hush!" snapped Horace.

"Am I speaking too loudly?" asked Sid.

"No, no."

Tad took his turn at questioning. "I understand you were governor of the South Quadrant. Very impressive."

"Are you offended by that?"

"Oh, no. All your staff had glowing recommendations," Tad said.

"They did?"

Horace turned to Tad; he nodded confidently. "I think we found our man."

"Should I go now? Are we through?"

"Yes, Sid," replied Horace. "Perfect timing. Good instincts. You're excused."

Sid surveyed the room. "Should I go out the same door I came in?"

"That should be fine," Tad assured him.

Sid paused and stepped further into the room. "Why are firemen here?" he asked blankly.

"Surveillance," Horace said jokingly.

"Oh." Sid blinked, sniffed cautiously and scurried from the library.

"Sid fits the bill perfectly!" stated Tad.

Horace looked over his shoulders. Inspector Oodles and Minnie smiled at him as they replaced the light switch plate. "Let's hope the installers are soon done," Horace said. "I have a few things to say in private."

THE DEBATE

Grand Auditorium at Groad University in Weaseldork was packed to capacity. The enormous sign suspended upstage summarized the event: *Battle for Icon of Groad*. In their quest to be elected, only four candidates remained. As the time to begin the telecast approached, each candidate readied themselves at their respective podiums.

Blade Watts was massaging his temples while humming an ancient resurrection tune. He wore a gray suit with a pink and green tie.

Lili Loath pranced about, jabbing the air like a boxer. Since this was a major Dazzle Box affair, her tattoo had been concealed. She wore a gray suit with a pink and green scarf.

Jake Hauser was having his podium cleaned with anti-bacterial spray. He kept repeating the instructions of his handlers, "Don't play with your dreadlocks. Look directly into the camera. Use one-syllable words." He wore a gray suit with a pink and green tie.

Zero was having a last minute snack—a plate of fried cheese balls—and flirting with Bella, the stage manager. He wore his pink and green suit.

"Places," announced Bella. "Thirty seconds to telecast!"

All the cameras were aimed at the moderator, Professor Spar, who took a sip of water, then realigned his name plate. The iridescent black-rimmed glasses were cosmetic. Professor Spar had perfect vision. His one-eyebrow raise, perfected after years of practice, always appeared spontaneous.

"Ten seconds to telecast!"

The audience ceased chattering.

". . . three . . . two . . . one!" Bella pointed to the professor.

"Hello. Welcome to the final national debate for Icon of Groad. I'm Professor Spar, anchor for TIHS. Let me explain the format for tonight's debate. Each candidate will give a one-minute opening air-fuse. Candidates will then respond to morose questions contorted by myself. Tonight's debate is sponsored by the Beleaguered Brood of Voters."

The warning lights, just out of camera range, began to flash. "Stand by, please." Professor Spar said. "It appears we have a technical problem."

Inspector Oodles and Minnie, dressed in technician coveralls, were making their way on stage. Minnie, wearing dark glasses and a feathered blond wig, whispered to three of the candidates who immediately removed their earpieces. When Zero offered his earpiece to Minnie, she refused him. Inspector Oodles, wearing a bald cap, distributed new ear devices to replace the confiscated ones. The imposter technicians nodded to the distinguished anchor and scurried off.

Professor Spar sighed with relief and continued. "It appears the devices which allow handlers to communicate to their candidates have malfunctioned, but they've been replaced. In the event you've just joined us, we're about to begin the final Icon debate which our sponsors have stupefyingly called the *Battle for Icon of Groad*. I'm the moderator for tonight's mayhem. I apologize for the brief delay. All technical problems have been solved and we are ready to begin."

Mr. Watts was the first to speak. "I'm Blade Watts, candidate from the *Crowbar Party*." He paused, assumed a dramatic posture, then spoke in a deeply serious tone. "Today is a critical moment in the life of Groad."

"Thank you," said Professor Spar. "Excellent." The Professor prompted Lili to speak.

"Hello. I'm Lili Loath, representing the *Sickle Party*." Her smile evaporated, replaced by a painful expression. "Our nation is at a road-cross," she uttered theatrically.

"Time's up!" announced Spar. "Next!"

"I'm Jake Hauser, member of the *Screwzer Party*." With masterful sensitivity, Jake duplicated the expression of a martyr he'd seen in a famous painting. "This is a defining moment for our country."

"Zip it," cracked Spar.

Jake was stunned. "That was a minute?!"

The Professor ignored the rebuff. "Your opening statement, Zero."

"I'm Zero with the *Ratchet Party*. I was born in Huckatash. Our family was poor. My mother was missing a leg. Every morning I hamstrung the papers, then walked seven miles to school. My first-grade teacher, Mrs. Nevers, taught me everything I know so I compress the value of an education. When I was twelve my uncle had the smallpox which scarred me for life. Life was a spin cycle of hard knocks. But I rose out of the maelstrom and now I'm running for Icon of Groad, the most pugnacious country in the orb, where dreams come true."

"Zero, you still have fifteen seconds," the Professor said.

"I married Maxie, a true hobby horse and we moved to Poshplum, which was renamed Drudgeville after our arrival. I inspired my father to start the privy business. I had a leg manufactured for my mother, who, for many years, walked with telescopes, before she crashed into herself and strolled away, leaving us in the dismals. My scars were removed with liposuction. Only in Groad. Where dreams come true!"

"My watch still shows five seconds, Zero."

"I inspired a privy business. I had a leg manufactured. I can do the same for our country."

"That concludes this portion of the debate." The Professor turned to another camera. "The candidates will now entertain a volley of shotgun questions. Jake, as Icon, what would be your primary agenda?"

Brimming with excitement, Jake shared his vision of a new world. "I will transform the army into a brigade of goodwill. We will subdue ground-quakes . . . overcome hydro-surges . . . grenade famines with food. I propose to bombard sickness with medicine. Rather than harpoon our enemies, we will lampoon them. Instead of dropping bombs on rogues we will write musical comedies about them. Generals will be awarded halos instead of stars!"

Stifling a gag, Professor Spar continued. "Miss Loath?"

"This is what I'm running against?" Lili asked of her opponent. "This is our country's brightest and best?"

"Your agenda, Miss Loath?" Spar said evenly.

Lili lit her own fuse. "The *Sickle Party* hopes to re-crackle the constitution. We need to shut our eyes and rewrite the entire document. We need a charter that allows us to build more fences, hurl larger projectiles, and un-fuse smelted couples! Return to the boom-boom days, that's my desire!"

Before Miss Loath could embark on an all-out tirade, Professor Spar interrupted. "Mr. Watts?"

"My comrades will work to harmonize the spirit of the rocks with the soul of the wind and dance with all ocean sprites so the mother essence can pirouette with the father force to create a harmonic orb where every child of the un-torched sky can sense his yin and yang in a full meaning of the idea."

The Professor grimaced. Next time he visited Doctor Waz, he decided, he would have his dose of antidepressants doubled. "Zero?"

"Without fail, I will lock up the boogeyman. Foremost, I'll send a Groad flag to every hungry child in the country. Furthermore, I'll widen the highways. In addition, the limit of speed shall be increased. Not to be outdone, the flow of money shall move faster. It is to be promised, every citizen shall observe good times. As requested, my portrait shall be distributed at every *GaggyMart.*"

The moderator was handed a sheet of paper. According to field surveys, less than one percent of the population of Groad was watching the debate. The Professor sighed. "We now move on to the fisticuffs round, where candidates are encouraged to pummel each other. Everyone, please put your notes aside and index up your sleeves." His address was interrupted by a shrill electronic sound followed by a buzzing noise. "Unfortunately," he said, "we are experiencing technical disturbances again. Step-ball-change with us. This sometimes happens at live broadcasts."

Lili Loath cocked her head. The voice in her earpiece had suddenly changed. It seemed she was no longer being prompted by her manager. She repeated aloud the message she just received. "Zero, could you respond to reports . . . ?"

Lili's question was carried along by Blade, ". . . That your Pa did not de-fizz from natural decay. . . ?"

Blade's comment was completed by Jake, ". . . But was, instead, murdered . . . ?"

Lili looked at Jake. "Pa Zero was murdered?"

Jake shrugged and spoke as instructed. "I give blood twice a week."

"I drained the blood from my jugular only once," announced Blade.

Jake, straining to hear the words in his earpiece, stuttered, "Pa Zero? The tycoon who owned a fleet of privies?" he asked. "Murdered?"

"Stabbed in the heart with a fork?!" Lili shouted.

"By his own son?" exclaimed Blake.

Jake looked into the wings. "I dine on humble pie."

"Children shouldn't fondle condoms," Blade blurted, recalling a lecture he'd heard in grade school.

Jake incorrectly repeated his signature campaign slogan. "Murderers will be awarded with halos."

Blade amplified his ear message. "Shout . . . why hasn't Zero been apprehended?"

Inspector Oodles and Minnie continued to feed the candidates rapid-fire comments, hoping to crack the circuitry of the automatons and turn them against one another. In the mayhem, surely Zero would divulge the truth.

"There is no record of my record," Jake admitted.

"We need to shut our eyes!" Lili screamed.

Jake stared at Blade. "Lili also murdered her Pa?"

Lili appeared dumbfounded, "A catastrophe is sometimes welcomed."

"Professor Spar, put an end to this!" begged Zero.

"We must slay diatribes and embrace the concept of digestion," declared Blade.

"Don't fandango with the flamingos," warned Lili.

Jake bellowed, "Lili has seven grinning skeletons in her boudoir!"

"Is *that* how Zero got his dings and dongs?" asked Lili in a brief moment of clarity.

Blade attempted to recite scripture. "Poverty is an evil. The love of dings and dongs is the root of all evil. Poverty is the love of dings and dongs."

"These allocations are outrageous!" howled Zero, thrashing the podium with his fists.

"Jake can't be trusted," stated Lili. "He says one thing to his enemies and the same thing to his friends."

"Fortunately, words are not apparent to the ear," muttered Blade.

"Cork the truth. Drink the lie," begged Lili.

Blade fired back. "A square peg was not meant to fit in a round hole!"

Jake proclaimed, "I only lie when it benefits me."

"I will not dignify my response with your answer!" swore Zero.

"I have, on occasion, *not* looked the other way," admitted Lili.

The Professor tried to interject. "Can we get back on agenda?"

Jake stepped forward. "I will initiate a tax invasion!"

Lili removed her shoes. "I promise to unplug the budget!"

Jake loosened his tie. "Zero, will you retain your Campaign Manager even if he's charged with embezzlement?"

"Move Pluto to provide shade from the sun," proposed Blake.

"Why did Hate marry Monger?" Jake asked.

Lili slapped her shoe against the podium. "Who will submit to a truth detector test?"

Jake removed his coat. "A patriot doesn't dance solo!"

"The weather has turned foul," Zero declared.

Lili announced, "The best trips are taken over time."

Blade pounded on the floorboards. "Can we down-tone the hysterics?"

Horace turned the volume on his headset up and instructed Zero to recite his list of campaign promises.

"The limit of speed shall be increased," Zero announced broadly.

"Zero, does your Vice Icon suffer from a mild form of rubber gears?" asked Jake.

"Dogs may become man's worst enemy!" shouted Zero.

"Blade is notorious for shaving profits off the sidewalk," insisted Lili.

"Lili is four-faced!" fired back Blade.

"Makeup should complement the disguise," hissed Jake, pointing at Lili.

"The cost of scum remover has skyrocketed."

Jake wagged his finger. "Blade speaks in six directions."

"I wear flat-footed, honest-to-ground shoes," Zero declared.

"Gravity is not an inherent right!" screamed Lili.

"Decay is an upkeep problem," Blade alleged.

Jake interrupted. "I support death only in concept."

Lili slapped her shoe against her chest. "Hurl larger projectiles! Hurl larger projectiles!"

"Zero, are the rumors about Maxie true?" demanded Blade.

Zero plowed ahead. "I will impose a tariff on all foreign automobiles."

Lili rallied. "Foreign Affairs paint themselves in boxes."

"I watch bedroom brawls with both binoculars," admitted Jake.

Lili raised her shoe overhead, "Think of yourself as my disciple!"

"I will not impose a tariff on all foreign autocrats," boomed Zero.

"Domestic policy increases with income."

"I file my income on the half shelf."

"What you see is an example of humane torture."

Zero, bobbing like a mechanical toy, spoke nonstop. "I repeat. I mean to say. I will impose a tariff on all foreign automobiles. I will *not* impose a tariff on all foreign autocrats. I *will* impose a tariff on all foreign automobiles."

"Could we have order?" pleaded Professor Spar.

Zero completed his diatribe, rewound, and started over. "I repeat. I will *not* . . ."

"EVERYONE, REMAIN CALISTHENIC!" shouted the Professor.

Zero's opponents spoke in unison. "ZERO, ANSWER THE QUESTION!"

"I will and will not impose a tariff . . ." Zero paused. "Horace," he begged to know, "what is a tariff?"

The Professor had turned purple. "Someone! Please. Punctuate the broadcast!"

Horace ripped off his headset and stepped out of the shadows. He picked up two connected cords and yanked with all his might. "Hell to handbaskets!" he muttered through his clenched teeth. The cords separated and Horace fell backwards. The auditorium went black.

THE INTERVIEW

The most popular Dazzle Box network in Groad was GOD, operated out of Weaseldork. GOD, a spin of the first, middle and last letters of Groad, had a long list of hits, including a popular morning show. Every weekday, precisely at seven AM, music was cued, the screen was flooded with a barrage of stirring images, and a voiceover artist, with an affectingly deep bass timbre, announced, "Hi. It's me. God. Welcome to *Good Morning, Groad*, a daily newscast devoted to serious issues affecting the orb, with your hosts, Paul and Appalling."

The host looked up and locked eyes with the camera. "Good morning. I'm Paul."

The hostess smiled, advertising everything that was perfect about her. "I'm Appalling. Glad you could join us."

Before addressing world events that affected millions of people, the couple discussed their own private dramas. "What's with the new hair architecture, Paul?" asked Appalling.

Paul delicately touched his reconditioned hair. "My stylist insisted. Do you like it?"

"More than like. It's hot," swooned Appalling. "Isn't it hot? Call the station and tell us what you think. Is Paul's hair up-do hot or not? We'll have the results tomorrow. By calling GOD you have an opportunity to win a million dongs. So call now!"

Paul artfully assumed a thoughtful expression. "Our first segment today features Zero, a contender for Icon."

"That's right, Paul," continued Appalling. "Zero's appearance is part of a series devoted to an in-depth look at each of the candidates."

"Zero will be accompanied by his wife, Maxie. I understand she just published a children's book entitled *Hog Tied*," announced Paul.

"That's correct, Paul. It's about a pig who's forced to repeat first grade over and over."

"Speaking of pigs," Paul interjected, "how are your children, Appalling?"

"Just astonishing! Kimmy is exfoliating and Tommy just began to cut teeth! Not his own, of course."

Paul was given the signal to move on by the floor manager. He leaned forward. "Before we meet Zero and Maxie, let's check with Tammy and get the morning headlines."

At another desk, a cheerful Tammy put down her cup of coffee. "Good morning, Paul, Appalling. Now . . . for the broken news. The Center for Health says those who park their brain in reverse may die from extinct diseases. Children are being placed on the Endangered Species List in the suburbs. The University of Hard Knobs is developing a smart bomb that targets stupidity. The Annual Ego Awards have been postponed due to an unprecedented number of applicants. The Secretary of State announced today he's in a coma. The production of honesty has declined due to low returns. The election is just two weeks away and, according to polls, Lili Loath remains the frontrunner. Back to you, Paul. And don't do a thing with the hair fountain!"

"Thank you, Tammy," Paul replied. He and his hostess settled down in an adjacent alcove, next to Zero and Maxie.

"Here we are with Zero and Maxie," Appalling stated.

Paul offered Zero a sympathetic look. "I'm sure it must be terribly nerve wracking as we enter the last days of the campaign?"

"As Tammy reported, you're a distant second in the polls," a sad-eyed Appalling reminded Zero, "but things could turn around, couldn't they?"

"We're wondering how you might do that," asked Paul. "What plans do you have to fight the huge wave of support Lili has marshmallow-ed behind her?"

"What do you say to critics who claim our country is headed for disaster?"

"Is Groad spinning out of control? Are we on the verge of doom?"

"Could we face an economic typhoon?"

"Are we a threat to ourselves? Will there be a ratatouille plague?"

"Is tragedy inevitable?"

"Can we overcome the horrors?"

"Do you predict a collapse?"

"What must we do to survive?"

"More with Zero and Maxie," announced Appalling, "when we return after these messages."

The Dazzle Box darlings immediately jumped up and scurried to the food cart where they helped themselves to sub-calorie coffee. Zero and Maxie remained on the sofa. Horace, who was observing the interview off camera, joined them.

"I think it's going really well," Maxie said.

Horace seemed pleased. "It's the best interview you've done, Zero."

"I agree," stated Maxie. "The best!"

Horace flashed Maxie a broad smile. "You look ravishing!" He quickly slapped Zero's knee. "Both of you!"

"How do I sound?" asked Zero.

"Perfect."

"You like what I have to say?"

"Don't change a thing," advised Horace.

Maxie lowered her voice. "I find Paul appalling but Appalling is appealing."

Horace shushed Maxie as the interviewers returned to their seats. He whispered into Zero's ear, "Surely our standing in the polls will go up because of this interview."

Appalling opened the segment. "Welcome back. We continue our in-depth conversation with Zero, who is running for Icon. Now, Zero, I know there's a story circulating that you were not, shall we say, the shiniest apple in school. So we contacted Mrs. Nevers, your first grade teacher, and she said, and I quote, 'I've never had a student on the level of Zero. Knowing what is expected of the typical Icon, I assure you, he is up to the job.' Unquote. That's so sweet. I'm wondering how you feel about Mrs. Nevers? It must be so touching to have her defend you in that way."

Like his co-host, Paul had also prepared a quote. "In addition to your intellectual pratfalls, there has also been concern about your physical condition. Are you capable of simonizing the job? We contacted your physician who sent this word gram." He read, "'I can a-sleuth that Zero has regular bladder flow, no mechanical organs, and is in full possession of his facilities.' I'd call that a clean receipt!"

"How do you answer your critics who say you nauseate the voters?" asked Appalling.

"Have you recovered from the last debate?" inquired Paul.

"Why won't those nagging droplets about your Pa go away?"

"Are you aware some people call you 'Saint?'"

"Have you contracted a carpenter to widen the doors of Icon Mansion should you win?"

"When will you learn the names of the leaders of other countries?"

"More with Zero and Maxie after this station break," announced Paul.

The stars of *Good Morning, Groad* rushed to refuel themselves with coffee. Maxie summoned Horace.

Zero was beaming. "The rails are greased. We're just steaming along!"

"I appreciate the fact you've finally learned to control your air valve," Horace said.

Maxie was chewing on a chunk of ice she'd fished out of a GOD mug. "Who would have thought a year ago we'd be here today, flapping on this show!"

"Maxie, I think it's time to upsize my suit again," announced Zero.

"It's time you put less chunkies down your blowhole!" snapped back Maxie.

Horace tapped the paper roll he'd stowed under his arm. "I'm sorry to report, once again, Lili Loath made the front page of the Ink Splotch."

"Where am I?" Zero wanted to know.

"Page ten," Horace informed him. "With the comics."

Zero pouted. "I don't like it when people aren't nice to me."

"We'll just have to find a way to overboard Lili," Maxie decided.

The hosts drained their cups and rejoined their guests.

"Welcome back," cooed Appalling, who'd planted herself next to Maxie. "We're having a very serious, very in-depth exchange with Zero and Maxie. Now, Maxie, I understand you wrote a children's book. I really admire people who have the ability to do that. It's such hard work. I wrote a children's book. Did you know that? It's called *Big People Who Irritate Me*. I want to read a section from your book, Maxie. The poor little pig's name is Hog. Is this an autobiographical account? We lived on a farm when I was growing up. I adore animals. So, let's read a page from my book, *Big People Who Irritate Me*." She opened her book, being sure to clearly display the cover. "'My Granny,'" she read, "'irritates me when she spreads butter on the wrong side of the toast.' What do you think of that? Clever, eh? Aren't the illustrations effervescent? If you become First Female and live in Icon Mansion will you sell my book in the gift shop?"

"That concludes our in-depth discussion," announced Paul. "Thanks, Zero and Maxie, for all your input. Let's go to Chuck Up for a report on the weather."

Without bidding their guests farewell, the hosts dashed off to be attended to by their makeup artists.

"Can't we just de-fizz Lili? Like we did Pa?" Zero asked Maxie.

"Hush!" she cried, unaware that Inspector Oodles had entered the studio.

The Inspector was dressed in a chauffeur's uniform. He wore sleek designer sunglasses, a perfect complement to his enormous bushy sideburns.

Horace pumped Maxie for the truth. "Why are you hushing Zero? I'm sure you dreamed of slugging old buzzard Lili, too."

"Of course" she said. "I'd wring the skull post of Lili Loath in a minute if I could."

When Horace saw the disguised Inspector he nearly jumped out of his skin. "Who are you?" he demanded.

"Hello. I am your chauffeur," replied Oodles. "Would you like to sashay back to the hotel?"

"Where's Leonardo?" asked Horace.

"He was instructed to undertake another assignment," explained Ooodles.

Horace shook his head. "Leonardo is our exclusive chauffeur!"

"What can I say? He is tied up," muttered Oodles. "I am excellent driver."

From across the studio, Appalling raised her voice. "Inspector Oodles! Is that you?!"

Oodles squinted in the direction of the speaker. "I beg your pardon!"

Appalling sprinted through the studio and threw her arms around Oodles. "What are you doing here?"

Oodles squirmed from her embrace. "I'm afraid you've mistaken me for someone else."

Appalling gave Oodles a playful slap. "I interviewed you. Remember? You were plugging your latest book, *Crime Crunching*."

"This man is an inspector?" asked Horace.

"One of the best!" cried Appalling.

Oodles backed off. "I must contradict you. Please. I go now." He saluted and bolted out the door.

Horace was stunned. "*Crime Crunching* you say?"

"It's a classic! Surely you've heard of it?" replied Appalling.

"Zero! Maxie!" Horace yelled. "Gather your spools. We're going to the bookstore to buy *Crime Crunching* and find out exactly who this imposter is!"

THE PARADE

Every autumn the City of Weaseldork sponsored Unity Parade. Groups from all over Groad gathered in the capital city and marched through its streets, proudly displaying their banners, promoting their causes, soliciting converts.

Zero had agreed to participate but was now unhappy about his decision.

"I wish you'd simmer up," sighed Maxie. "It's a ducky day for a parade. You get to strut your carcass."

"I don't see the sense of it! In this scorchy sun, I'll wither like a porky dog," complained Zero.

Horace reminded him, "It would be political suicide not to participate."

"This is the day every group in Groad marches together to hooray our epoxy as a country," explained Maxie.

"I don't give a jot for epoxy," muttered Zero.

"If you back out, you will be labeled a de-clubber, and a parade pooper," threatened Horace.

From a side street, LeRoy Strun appeared, pulling a rickshaw. "Mr. Zero," he declared, "I'm LeRoy. I'll be pulling you down Groad Avenue."

"You want me to nestle in that contraption?" cried Zero. "I'd rather sidle down the street on my own two feet!"

"Oh, Zero," Maxie cracked. "Do be reasonable. There is no way you can trundle your carcass over a three-mile-long parade route."

LeRoy had a small constellation of freckles on the left side of his forehead that resembled a snowflake. He smelled like a bar of recently unwrapped sandalwood soap. The rickshaw was decorated with items LeRoy had found on the beach while treasure hunting with his metal detector. A necklace and pair of bracelets, brimming with dangling seashore findings glinted in the sunlight.

Horace studied LeRoy for a long moment. "Would you look sideways?" he said. Horace closely examined LeRoy's profile and compared it to photographs in *Crime Crunching*. "Now face front," he instructed. Again, Horace flipped through the book, occasionally pausing to study the photographs.

LeRoy was growing uncomfortable. "Is something wrong?"

"Is that nose real?" asked Horace.

LeRoy frowned. "Yes. Of course, sir."

Horace looked up LeRoy's nostrils. "It looks phony. Like a rubber plug. A polished rubber plug."

LeRoy stepped back. "This is my come-out-of-womb look. I swear!"

"Oh, relax, Horace," cried Maxie. "LeRoy is not Inspector Oodles."

"We can't be too careful," admonished Horace.

"Is that *Crime Crunching* by Inspector Oodles?" asked LeRoy.

Horace was taken aback. "Yes."

"I love that book!" exclaimed LeRoy.

"Do you know Inspector Oodles showed up, interrogating Zero, dressed in some of the very same disguises found in this book!"

"No!"

"And," Horace added, "if I'm not mistaken, he'll show up today."

LeRoy was overjoyed. "You think so!? I'd love his autograph!"

A young woman with crutches and a black eye approached the quartet as they waited for the parade to begin. "Could I have a moment, Zero? I'm Claudia Falls, a representative of *Siblings Against Rivalry*."

Instantly Horace consulted *Crime Crunching*, determined to discover if she were an undercover agent.

"Claudia?" pleaded Zero, "would you scratch my dorsal? Don't be afraid to dig in. Use your claws."

For Claudia it was the perfect opportunity. She was able to pleasure Zero while showing him the official button of *Siblings Against Rivalry*. "Just for the parade, would you wear this token supporting our cause?"

"If it gets the sibling vote," replied Maxie, "he'll do it."

Claudia ran her nails along the spine of Zero. He began to purr. "I also work for *Actors with Broken Femurs*," she said. "I brought their armband with me. Wearing it would expose their plight."

Zero recoiled. "I never gave a logjam for actors! No!"

"Oh, hush!" cried Maxie. "We need every vote we can get. Even from stage-strutters." She wrapped the band around his arm, binding the ends with a hair pin.

"So as not to offend musicians," continued Claudia, "I brought a sash for *Singers with Cut Throats*."

Maxie sighed. "If it brings victory, we'll endorse anything." She slipped the sash over Zero's shoulder.

All along, Horace had suspected Claudia was a man. He finally summoned up the courage to ask, "Are those pointers real?"

"Sir!" exclaimed Claudia, "I will not tolerate harassment of any form, you pecker-pusher." She swatted the Campaign Manager with a crutch and hobbled off, shouting, "I'm going to start a women's group *Impale Patriarchal Perverts!*"

Zero surveyed the sky. "When does this parade start?"

"Will you lactate!" cried Maxie.

"What is Lili Loath riding in?" Zero asked LeRoy.

"She was assigned a surrey."

"And Jake? What is his mode of transport?"

"A scooter."

"Blade? What contraption was assigned to him?"

"A coaster."

Zero glared at LeRoy. "Why didn't I get a surrey?"

"Zero, oh, Zero! Please! Would you do me a favor?" The trio turned to find a woman standing next to them. The suppliant was strikingly beautiful, with crazed eyes. "My name is Angie." She offered Zero a bag. "Would you throw these favors to the spectators?"

Poor Horace sifted through the pages of *Crime Crunching* once again.

"Something to eat?" asked Zero.

"Charms." Angie's pupils dilated. "Gifts from *The Zealots*."

Maxie was ready to comply. "*The Zealots* are a powerful loud group who can garner lots of votes. Say yes, Zero!"

Horace interrupted. "No! If you favor *The Zealots* you'll offend *The Fanatics*, who will retaliate by voting for the candidate backed by *The Hysterics*!" He gave Angie a push. Happily, she didn't resist but floated down the street, blithely flinging about her charms.

"The parade's about to begin," announced LeRoy. "Perhaps you should get in the carriage."

Maxie needed reassurance. "Let me see your wave." Zero responded with a formal wave. "Very nice. Don't ever stop! Wave. Smile. Throw lip. This is being broadcast all over Groad!"

His entry into the carriage was followed by two loud popping sounds. "Hell and damnation!" he shouted. "The wheel's have collapsed. What are we going to do now?"

"I'm sure I can pull you. Even with horizontal tires," said LeRoy.

Maxie kissed LeRoy on the lips. "You're a sugar beet."

"Sugar?" Zero looked around, anticipating sweets.

A pair of females, dressed in matching outfits, skipped up. They wore box-pleated skirts and high top socks. They carried matching flags, wore miniature pompoms in their hair and sported back saddle shoes. "Go, Unity Parade," Inspector Oodles exclaimed, hooking pinkie fingers with Minnie. They curtsied.

"Hello, girls!" cried Zero.

Horace intercepted. "Not so close!" he warned the twins.

Inspector Oodles and Minnie spoke in unison. "We're here to escort Zero."

Horace studied the ladies intently. "Nobody mentioned escorts. Who sent you?"

"Why, the *Ratchet Party*, of course," sighed Oodles. He unfurled the flag to clearly reveal the *Ratchet Party* logo. "My name is Thelma."

"They do add pomposity to the occasion," Maxie said gleefully.

Oodles pointed to his cheerleading partner, "This is Theona."

Zero regretted there wasn't room enough in the rickshaw for the twins. "I'd offer you a seat, but it's been excavated."

"Zero, are you strapped in?" asked LeRoy.

Theona smiled at Horace. "I see you have *Crime Crunching*. Do you like it?"

"No," Horace replied coldly.

Theona bit her lip. "Were I to meet Inspector Oodles, I'd . . ."

"Yes?"

"I'd . . . volunteer . . . to crunch . . . crime with him," she confessed slyly.

Horace gave Oodles the once over. "What did you say your name was?"

"Thelma."

"Thelma," Horace repeated, not taking his eyes off the mysterious creature.

"Are you flirting with me?" asked Oodles.

"Horace! Behave!" barked Maxie.

Theona puckered her lips. "Have you taken a shine to my twin Thelma?"

Horace, overcome with Thelma's charms, blushed.

Maxie whacked Horace on the behind with her purse. "Keep your eyes outward, you double looker!" She turned to Thelma, "My charms are broader than yours, you ingrate!" She swung the purse, but Oodles ducked and Maxie tumbled to the pavement. "Zeus almighty!" she screamed.

Horace knelt by Maxie. "My titter-tot, have you fractured yourself?"

"I threw out my hip!" she cried. "Align me, Horace!"

"Un-kink you? How?"

Maxie raised a leg. "Pull!"

Horace was reluctant. "I don't wish to undo your connectors."

"Just pull! Rotract my limbs!" screamed Maxie. Horace obeyed. There was an earsplitting pop. After a moment, the restored Maxie sat up. "Thank you. Could you rub my disinfected joint?"

The twins, meanwhile, were eagerly anticipating how their latest plan to undo Zero would unfold. "Just wait until Zero sees the trussed-up manikin we planted in the crowd—a perfect replica of his Pa!" whispered Oodles.

Minnie clapped her hands gleefully, "When laying eyes upon the visage of his Pa, Zero will cease to breathe."

"'A ghost!' Zero will proclaim. 'Pa Zero back from the dead to have his revenge.'"

"The blood will drain from his knob."

"Zero will fall to the ground. A sack of porridge."

"We'll remove the vials from our hollow flag staffs," said Minnie.

"Mine has silly salts!"

"Mine contains star dust!"

"You'll sprinkle his eyes with dust. I'll hoist the salts under his nose," instructed Oodles.

"When he awakens, he'll be floating on a froggy dream cloud!" exclaimed Minnie.

Oodles patted his chest, "I'll say, 'Welcome to the hereafter!'"

"I'll say, 'Which will it be, Zero? The pearly gates? Or the gates of peril?'"

"'Unless you confess your crimes, Zero, it's the torture pit for you!'"

"And I shall capture every foul, blundering word on the voice trap!" exclaimed Minnie.

Horace separated the twins. "What are you two whiskering about?" he asked, patting them on their heads. When he withdrew his hand, he accidentally pulled the wig from Oodles head.

"Oh, my leprechaun!" cried Maxie.

"I should have known!" exclaimed Horace. "Inspector Oodles!"

"Don't be absurd," replied Oodles. "I'm Thelma."

Horace searched the crowd for a policeman. "Someone! Arrest this man!"

Oodles viced Horace in a skull hold. "Why would I pretend to be Oodles?"

"Don't Oodle me," muttered Horace. "I've seen photographs!" He slipped from Oodles' grasp.

Oodles turned tricks. "I'm Arnie Brewster," he announced.

"Arnie Brewster?" Horace whispered hoarsely.

"Who's he?" asked Maxie.

"No one," Horace answered. "A made-up name. A fictional clod."

"Arnie Brewster," Oodles repeated, nodding his head.

Zero crinkled his brow. "Arnie? Isn't he the sniveler named in Pa's will?"

Horace gasped and turned to LeRoy. "You with the cart. Take Zero somewhere else. Go!"

Maxie stared at the wigless Oodles. "Would someone explain!"

Oodles kissed Minnie. "Did you hear? Zero confessed. Pa Zero's dongs really belong to me!"

"Zero said no such thing!" screamed Horace.

"Give me that book!" demanded Maxie, pulling it out from under Horace's arm.

"You can't trust a word Zero says!" Horace warned Oodles.

Maxie tried to set Horace straight. "This man is lying! He isn't Arnie Brewster." She held up the book. "He's Inspector Oodles!"

"Guilty as charged," replied Oodles.

"Where did the name Arnie Brewster come from? Who is he?" demanded Maxie.

"Arnie Brewster," confessed Oodles, "Is my client."

THE SHAKEDOWN

Despite a rousing reception at Unity Parade, Zero was unable to raise his numbers in the polls. Horace decided, therefore, it was time to bang heads and reassess their tactics. All the primary players had gathered at Zero's Campaign Headquarters in the basement of Mollie's Meathouse in Weaseldork.

"What is that upstairs noise!?" asked Cleo, the wife of Sid, now the official candidate for Vice Icon of Groad.

"That's Smelt and Clink, keeping lookout," replied Horace.

"Who are they?"

"We are the brains of the campaign," Horace explained. "Smelt and Clink are the muscle. They worked next door, in the slaughterhouse, before we hired them. Very beefy. You'll meet them, I'm sure."

Maxie winked at Cleo. "You'll love them. You'll never see a finer cut of meat."

Horace summarized their situation, "We just can't seem to pull out of the slump we're in."

Sid was clueless. "Why is that?" he asked.

Maxie was clearly frustrated. "The political shit-fans said Zero won the debate!"

Sid reminded everyone, "Zero was awarded *The Actors Quarantine* for his commercial." He noticed everyone in the room turn to him in astonishment. "Wasn't he?" he added.

Horace mused, "There for a minute I really thought you had composed a declarative sentence, Sid."

"I need to work on that, don't I?" Sid replied.

Maxie expressed her desire to hurl a handful of darts at Lili. "Every day that shrew seems to climb a notch in the polls!"

Horace offered his analysis. "I attribute it to Lili's running mate. He's very charismatic and exceedingly dim."

"What's to be done?" asked Zero.

Maxie aimed her question squarely at Horace. "Any word from Inspector Oodles or his client Arnie Brewster?"

"I keep telling you, Maxie, there is no such man as Arnie Brewster!" he shouted.

The wife of Sid, Cleo, spoke. "I say we fryball Lili! As to her running mate . . . that pretty boy suck face . . . douse him with acid! Get me the carbonate. I'll do it myself!" Cleo extinguished her cigarette, mashing the burning stub in the palm of her hand.

Horace waited until Cleo settled down. "Actually, Cleo, we think your husband is an even greater problem."

"Me?" squawked Sid.

Zero was equally eager to blame his vice mate. "You're the cause of our woes. Because of you, we're losing."

"What's wrong with me?" pondered Sid.

"I find you loud, disagreeable, demanding and altogether obnoxious!" snarled Zero.

Cleo began to twist the mole on her chin. "My Sid is the perfect running mate! He never says a word. He applauds your speeches and maintains a perfect six-point carat smile."

"Bull testicles!" Zero pounced back. "Who really believes . . . when I am Icon . . . that Sid could carry on my legacy, were I to die?"

"I assure you," Cleo said, her words crisp and measured. "His tenure would be a continuation of the Zero program."

Maxie chimed in. "I agree with Zero. Sid is a sloth. It's time he faced the boot."

"If I'm fired, who will you pick as Vice Icon?" asked Sid.

"Me!" cried Maxie. "I fit the foot brilliantly. Keep it in the family, I say."

Zero clapped. "A toxic idea! I like it."

"A husband and wife governing the country?" exclaimed Sid. "Has that ever been done?"

Horace dismissed Sid's concern. "Many times. Just not officially."

"If Maxie is Vice Icon, who will be First Female?" asked Cleo.

"Don't fret about that, kitten. I'll find someone," promised Zero.

Sid appealed to his wife. "Sweetie, can't you do something?"

"Face it, Sid. You're a political sinkhole," Horace concluded.

Like a cornered bulldog, Cleo stood. She pinched off the top button of her blouse, her face flushed with fury. "Now you sit down and listen to me! Sid and I contributed millions of dongs to this campaign. Don't say a word! The man started with nothing! He made his fortune, ding by ding. Despite his past! His grandmother migrated from Primordia, where she was prohibited from advancing past her epoch. She married a foreigner and give birth to an accent—Sid's father—who became a victim of horrific verbal profiling. On the other side, his grandfather, a Bottom-Feeder, was teased mercilessly for his means of employment. He married a Free-Roller and subsequently was abused by the Anti-Boomers. Their daughter—Sid's mother—could not find her archetype and endured untold hardships. So it should be clearly apparent, HORACE, that SID REPRESENTS ALL THE RUNTY PEOPLE OF GROAD! Without him, any chance of a comeback will frizzle. Do you want to do that? Alienate EVERY Free-Roller, Anti-Boomer, Bottom-Feeder, Retro-Goon, Accent-Victim, and

Brain-Bender in this country? He's their mascot, damn it!" She grabbed the map of Groad in her fist and ripped it from the wall.

Horace fired back. "There are so few Brain-Benders in Groad their votes are negligible!"

"Despite Sid's long, admirable lineage, Cleo, Sid does not inspire hysteria," Maxie stated. "It's time to cut him loose."

Sid was near tears. "What will I do?"

Zero flashed Sid a crooked smile. "Why not be my bodyguard? A few pellets and you'll grow a nice, thick skin."

"Your bodyguard?" gasped Sid.

"Am I not worth protecting? You would not die for me?"

"The idea!" bellowed Cleo.

"Most people would consider it an honor," gushed Zero, "to shield a man of my stature."

Sid turned to his wife. "Sweetie, can you tell Zero, 'No'?!"

"Oh!" cried Zero, "you consent to be my running mate, but not serve as my bodyguard?"

Maxie jumped on board. "That shows his true character."

"Will you resign peacefully, or must we whack it out of you?" asked Zero.

"Zero," Cleo threatened, "if you torch Sid, I'll hang your mucky underwear out for the whole orb to see!"

Maxie gasped. "You wouldn't dare!"

Cleo smirked. "There is nothing worse—for politicians—than to have their incontinence exposed."

Sid snickered. "Can you imagine the tabloids?"

Cleo shook her bosom. "The comedians will make you the laughing stock of Groad!"

An emboldened Sid shook the room with epitaphs. "*The Hysterics* will re-puke your nappy! Among Anti-Boomers you'll be known as a soiler! *The Zealots* will dis-o-bowel you! *The Fanatics* will spread rumors of your colonoscopies!"

"Horace! Zero! Do something!" cried Maxie.

Zero shrugged off the threats of Sid and Cleo. "I will not marmalize my values. My mind is wedged to Horace's. Sid goes, and you, my chucky chops, Maxie, are my new Vice Icon."

THE SCAM

The law office of Mr. Bucket was furnished with solid mahogany furniture and gold accessories. Once a workhorse, the attorney now considered it an imposition to work more than two hours a week. That Mr. Bucket was at his office on this particular Friday afternoon was only a coincidence. He'd stopped by simply to sign an enormous check his secretary wished to deposit before the weekend.

A visitor approached the attorney's open door, ringing a small pagoda bell she carried with her. "Dr. Bucket?" she whispered.

The attorney looked up to correct the speaker. "C. K. Bucket, Certified Master of Jurisprudence." He observed a beautiful, coy woman dressed in a kimono.

"What a fancy name you have?" tittered Minnie.

Mr. Bucket pushed his pen aside. "I make, interpret, massage, or ignore the law. Whatever you wish."

"Have you a minute?" asked Minnie coquettishly.

"For you, madam," replied Mr. Bucket, "I have all afternoon . . . and a reclining couch . . . Please sit. Don't hide your charms. It's against the law!"

Minnie performed a slow half-bow, "You are kind to me."

"What's on your mind? inquired Mr. Bucket. "Let's undress it, shall we?"

Minnie was wide-eyed. "I have a problem."

"Nothing I can't solve, I'm sure."

Minnie dropped her voice. "I want a divorce."

"That's easily done," admitted Mr. Bucket. "We'll negotiate the terms over dinner."

"Not so quick!" cried Minnie.

"Of course. A bit of foreplay first," Mr. Bucket suggested.

"My husband is rich," she confided.

The attorney leaned forward. He rested his elbows on the desk. "Would that be rich or very rich?"

Minnie studied the pattern on the ceiling. "Very rich, I think. But he won't give me dings."

"We'll change that," promised Mr. Bucket.

Minnie sighed with relief. "Then I need not fear? Divorcing him will not impoverish me?"

The attorney smiled. "Embrace me as your counselor. You'll be showered with riches. From all directions."

"Sushi!" someone called from the lobby.

"Oh! That's my husband!" cried Minnie. "How did he learn my aboutswhere?"

She closed the door and leaned against it.

"I know you're in there! Dr. Bucket. I wish to see my wife," Inspector Oodles demanded, pounding on the door.

"He must not see me," pleaded Minnie.

"I'm not a patient man! Open the door!"

"Perhaps I hide in your vault?" Minnie suggested.

Mr. Bucket shook his head. "I keep my files there."

Minnie clasp her hands together. "I won't touch a thing, won't make a squeak of noise."

"Only a minute," agreed Mr. Bucket. He walked to the door while she scurried into the vault. When she closed the steel-bar gate behind her, Mr. Bucket admitted the impatient husband.

"Bucket," Oodles cracked. "What kind of contemptible name is that? Hand her over!" The Inspector was dressed in formalwear. He had thick glasses and an old fright wig. The battery to a large old-fashioned hearing aid was tucked in his vest pocket; its earpiece cord dangled behind him, dragging on the floor. He commandeered a walking stick.

Bucket pleaded innocence. "I am alone, sir! And if you don't leave immediately, I'll file an unlawful entry suit against you!"

"Which will be answered with a kidnapping subpoena," cracked Oodles. "Where did you stash her, you perv?"

"Add slander to the list of charges!"

"Did the floozy tell you I have lots of dongs? Uh? Yes, I see she did. It's a lie."

"There's been a mistake," Mr. Bucket said. "I'm sure your wife is waiting for you at home."

Oodles disagreed. "I know the aboutswhere of my wife, sir. Her maid keeps me informed."

"Bribery and suspected blackmail of a servant," Mr. Bucket noted.

Oodles abruptly changed his mood. He clutched his heart. "My Sushi wants a divorce."

"Do you need representation?"

Oodles began to weep. "I don't understand. We had such a good marriage. Exchanged vows just a week ago."

"I'm sorry." Mr. Bucket said weakly.

"Listen," pleaded Oodles. "I'm not going to live much longer. If you keep me waiting, I may de-fizz in your office. Where's Sushi? I miss my little scrunchie."

"I can't bear it any longer," Minnie whimpered as she rushed from the vault. "The pain in your voice. Did I cause your little pipsqueak heart to palpitate? I'm sorry, honey."

Oodles received the contrite Minnie warmly. "Sushi. Give me a peck and a roll."

Minnie apologized to Mr. Bucket. "I'm sorry to bother you. I will hold onto our marriage."

"Good luck. Here's my card." Mr. Bucket winked. "I'm an expert shaver of law."

"Did you find Pa Zero's will?" Oodles asked Minnie as they exited the law office.

"Yes," she replied.

"Where is it?" asked Oodles.

Minnie giggled. "I dare you to find it."

The Inspector studied Minnie, a gleam in his eye. Suddenly, he kissed his assistant on the mouth. When he regained his senses, he withdrew. "Simply playing the part of your husband," he explained. "Your pretend husband!"

THE FALLOUT

The beams of Mollie's Meathouse basement seemed to be crumbling under the weight of misfortune. A dejected Horace leafed through the reports compiled by the Party's Intelligence Committee. Cleo, Sid's wife, had kept her word. Every day the Dazzle Box would broadcast new, damaging allegations about Zero. Every day the Ink Splotches printed corrosive stories. All spread by Cleo.

"What are they saying?" asked Zero.

"Pay them no divinity."

Zero persisted. "Horace, tell me."

"Don't fret yourself," sighed Horace. "There will always be discontents who find you irksome."

"Who are these discontents?"

"Disagreeable, quagmire people who wish to torpedo the campaign," replied Horace. "So, they spread the vexing lies of that vengeful Cleo."

Zero slammed his fist on the cutting table. "Make a list! Who's quoting Cleo? Who has been slandering my carcass? I want names!"

"Herb Blowhob, for one," Horace said, smacking a side of beef hanging from the rafters. "For days and days that yak-jaw has been spouting nasty verbiage about you on the airwaves."

"He says you're a flip-flop-flapper, a woeful promise breaker, a vile reptile," relayed Maxie.

Zero shrugged. "Which politician isn't?"

"That's not all," stated Horace. "Herb Blowhob says you snuffed your Pa, then pillaged his bank account, obtaining billions of dongs illegally."

"That's a cow of a different udder," cried Zero. "Where are Smelt and Clink?"

"Upstairs. Drinking protein sides and flossing their muscles," replied Horace.

Zero pushed aside a bone saw and waddled to the stairwell. "Clink! Smelt!" he yelled. "Get down here!"

The thugs appeared at the top of the stairs. "Hey, boss."

"Is someone causing Zero trouble?" asked Clink. "You need us to de-glam someone?"

"Find Herb Blowhob," instructed Zero. "Crunch his knuckles in a vice and extrude the man's sausages."

Horace was ready to add more names to the list. "What about Mr. Artoe? Should Clink and Smelt visit him?"

Zero frowned. "Artoe? Who's he?"

"He writes a weekly column for *The Bugle*," explained Horace. "He's a flimflammer. Though he galloped for years in the army, he claims you're not qualified to be Icon because you never cavorted in the military."

"Hogwash! I fought in endless wars and was awarded hordes of medals!"

Smelt was impressed. "You did?!"

"I'll be sock-darned," muttered Clink.

"I was also awarded a Varicose Vein in the Great War against Logic," boasted Zero.

Clink spit. "Really?!"

"Furthermore," trumpeted Zero, "I was given a Moonshine for stoking fires during the Invasion of Absurdity!"

Smelt grabbed Zero's hand and shook it vigorously. "I'm stupefied!"

"But Mr. Artoe says those are faux medals, Zero," pined Horace.

"Smelt. Clink. Re-size Mr. Artoe. Grommet his tongue. Mince his thumbs. Remove his tattoos. Make sure the puss-pot never speaks or writes again!"

The duo flexed their muscles. "Yes, sir!"

"Anyone who disparages me, de-hunk him," Zero commanded, "I won't have Cleo or Lili or anyone else squander our dreams with their sorcery. I will win this election fair and squares."

Maxie was cheering. "Oh, Zero! That's my puffy loon! Sometimes your crusty qualities really do come through."

"Interesting," Horace muttered under his breath.

Maxie froze. "What?"

"This report," answered Horace. "On the latest polls."

"Speak up," growled Zero.

There was a strange tone in Horace's voice. "There's been a change."

Maxie sighed knowingly. "Lower than yesterday? Oh, dear."

"No," Horace said disbelievingly.

Maxie planted her fists firmly on her hips. "Well?"

"Our numbers have gone up," whispered Horace. "Incredible!"

"Really?"

Horace nodded. "By quite a bit."

"How could that be?" demanded Maxie. "There have been so many egregious reports about Zero."

"Lili, meanwhile, dropped ten points."

"Zero!" cried Maxie. "Maybe things are turning around."

Horace was puzzled. "Why? What's the pump behind the change?"

Maxie rolled her pelvis. "Don't forget. I'm now the candidate for Vice Icon. My presence on the ticket caused the bounce, I'd say."

"I doubt that's the reason," said Horace.

Maxie socked him. "The nerve! I'm getting tired of all your little under-arm nips."

"Perhaps," surmised Zero, "the reports of Cleo are attributed to Lili. Loathsome Lili, they decided, is waltzing in dirty politics. And the people of Groad despise dirty politics!"

Horace contemplated the idea.

"It's a thought," Maxie said.

"A pineapple thought, indeed." Horace smiled. "I must give this further consultation."

THE TALLY

On the evening of election day, all key members of the *Ratchet Party* had assembled in the grand ballroom of Swanky Hotel. The crowd included supporters of Zero's bid for Icon, as well as potential employees, were Zero to win. The room was decorated with pink and green streamers, balloons, posters and flags. There was no limit to the amount of loopy juice flowing from taps. In a corner of the room, Smelt and Clink, shirtless, had set up a feeding station, carving up slices of rare roast beef, impaling the meat with miniature Groad flags, serving them to the amused guests.

A temporary media center had been set up in the foyer. It was equipped with telephones, facsimile machines, emergency call boxes, and a collage of Dazzle Box screens.

Horace was nervous. "This is it! The final down-count. The polls are closed. Results are coming in."

Mr. Bucket surveyed the latest tally sheet. "Initial numbers are looking good," the attorney announced, "Zero has a substantial lead."

Maxie, who'd convinced Marcus Marko to design another dress for this event, fluttered through the crowd, flaring her skirt at every turn. "Horace," she cried, "Your plan worked! We barraged the media with the nastiest, most un-glorious stories about Zero all the while blaming Lili for sowing them!" She flashed a deliciously sour smile and floated off.

"Order more food!" cried Zero.

Wanda, Manager of *Shimmer Clinic*, spoke up, "It was a brilliant campaign!"

Head of *Consolidated Energy*, Miss Greedo, joined the chorus, "A most honest campaign!"

Although Mr. Bucket had lost the ability to smile long ago, he forced a stiff grin. "I look forward to providing un-legal counsel throughout your Icon-hood, Zero."

Miss Greedo plucked a card from a fanfare of flowers, one of many bouquets perched on tables throughout the ballroom. "Look at this complimentary note. It reads, 'Which candidate do I trust? Zero!' Isn't that the sweetest!"

Maxie snatched the note from an arrangement of tomato stalks and read, "'Who has a grasp of the issues? Zero!' What a delirious sentiment!"

From a vase of thorny isotopes Wanda grabbed a card that read, "'Who represents my values? Zero!'" She pretended to wipe away a tear. "Groad has such kind, thoughtful people!"

Horace plucked a sheet of paper from the tray of a facsimile machine. He studied the numbers. "With fifty percent tabulated, Zero is leading, two to one!"

"Oh, Horace," sighed Maxie. "Let me snuggle you." She wrapped her arms around Horace and pinched his butt-chops.

Zero was unhappy with the results. "Forty percent refusing to vote for me? After I'm sworn in, we'll hunt down those traitors! Until everyone in Groad swears allegiance to me, our work is not done!"

"In our business that's what we call consolidating!" Miss Greedo chopped. "These are exhilarating times. Zero, keep me in mind for Energy Secretary!" She turned to the head of *Shimmer Clinc*, "Wanda, dear, be a turnip, would you, and pour me another loopy?"

Mr. Bucket stood on a table, calling for everyone's attention. "Since we're all in such a chipper mood, I have to say this: I never passed the bar exam!"

"Eighty percent reporting and Zero is still leading, two to one," Horace announced over the public address system. "There's no way we can lose now."

"Another loopy!" cried Maxie.

Miss Greedo climbed onto the counter. "As long as we're confessing secrets. I sometimes swath my body in a cheese wrap and let the dogs lick me off."

Wanda grabbed the microphone from Horace and broadcast her daring, heinous crime. "Did anybody ever make tea from old used bags and serve it to their guests? I do!"

The room grew silent for a moment, during which Mr. Bucket yelled, "A telegram from Lili!" He handed the paper to Horace.

Horace read, "'After weeks of turd-slinging and frothing of the mind, the citizens of Groad have spoken. I concede. The winner is Zero. Congratulations!'"

"I won! I won! I won!" cried Zero, dancing in circles.

Maxie planted a wet kiss on Horace's lips. "Well done!" she whispered.

"Heavens below, Maxie, dear," exclaimed Zero. "Why are you locking lips with Horace? I'm the winner!"

Maxie ignored her husband. "This is a pinky day, if ever there was one! When do we occupy Icon Mansion?"

"Not for another month," Horace reminded her.

"Before moving in, the election must be vilified," said Smelt.

"It won't be a problem," promised Clink. "We'll see to that."

"I'm going to paint the whole damn mansion pink. Inside and out!" screamed Maxie.

Inspector Oodles, dressed in the attire of his profession, entered, wearing a trench coat. Minnie, who carried two Tommy guns, accompanied him.

"The shenanigans are over," Oodles announced.

"Inspector Oodles!" cried Horace.

Maxie sighed dramatically. "Again! What is the Inspector worming for now?"

Miss Greedo stumbled over to Minnie and offered her a drink. "Miss, could you not skank those guns about?"

"You're under arrest, Zero!" Oodles stated.

"Impossible!" cracked Zero. "I've never in my life committed a crime."

Inspector Oodles narrowed is eyes. "I think Arnie Brewster will disagree."

"That name again!" exclaimed Maxie. "Who is Arnie? Will someone please tell me?!"

Oodles held up Pa Zero's will. "Arnie Brewster is Pa Zero's second son. A bastard child he favored *very very* much. His *lawful* heir!"

Horace attempted to snatch the paper from Oodles' hand. "Where did you get that?"

"My assistant secured it from the vaults of Mr. Bucket, your attorney," replied the Inspector.

Horace turned to Mr. Bucket. "You said you destroyed that!"

"No lawyer in his right mind would trash any item that could be used for extortion or blackmail!" argued Mr. Bucket.

Minnie raised her guns. "Hopefully, now, Arnie will receive the money intended for him."

"We all have family spats," Maxie said apologetically. "That's no reason to arrest Zero. We'll gladly share the lard with Arnie . . ."

"Pa Zero's will was forged with the blessing of Zero," explained Oodles. "That's a felony. An accused felon is not allowed to serve as Icon."

"I'M ICON! I PUKE THE LAW!" bellowed Zero.

Inspector Oodles put up his hand. "Vetoed!"

"I didn't forge anything," Zero blubbered. "It was Horace!"

"It was Bucket!" yelled Horace.

"I plead the seventh!" snapped Mr. Bucket.

Minnie looked at Oodles. "Sounds like a conspiracy to me, Inspector."

Oodles nodded but wished to clarify one point. "I presume Maxie, not being familiar with Arnie Brewster and the phony will, is innocent."

"The dame gets off this time," agreed Minnie.

"We solved the riddle of the will. As to the death of Pa Zero, we're still collecting evidence. He had a cacophony of dings and dongs. That makes for a powerful motive to have him de-fizzed," reasoned Oodles.

"You can't prove anything!" Horace cracked.

"It was Zero!" Maxie confessed. "Zero was the one who murdered him. With muck fumes."

"That . . . I call evidence!" Oodles snapped handcuffs on Zero.

"Why am I being trap-snapped like this?" asked Zero.

"I'm sorry, Sugar Lumps," uttered Maxie.

"I'm being carted to prison?" cried Zero.

"Don't stroke yourself," said Maxie soothingly. "Remember. I'll be Icon. I'll see that your carcass is treated with utmost abrasion!"

"The situation outside is sweltering," reported Clink. "There's a rabble of photographers waiting to snap a picture of you, boss"

"My wife. Replacing me?" sobbed Zero. "Robbing me of my triumph?! But it was Maxie's idea to de-fizz the old man," he cried. "She's responsible. She's the crook! My poor dear curvaceous heart!"

"Pipe down!" hissed Maxie. "Put on a gleeful face for the photographers."

"How did this happen?!" Zero cried as he was escorted outside. "Maxie is the guilty one! I'm not a crook! I'm Zero! I'm Zero! I'm Zero! I'm Zero!"

"Sad," concluded Horace. "He really was the perfect politician."

"The poor bloke," Clink muttered, wiping his eye. "Zero was riding the rocket to infinity . . ."

"Immortality," Smelt corrected. "You mean immortality. Or is it immorality . . . ?"

Ignoring Smelt, Clink continued. "Then, a tragic fall-down. From infinity . . . to zero."

ACKNOWLEDGEMENTS

Zero began as a play—*Zero to Infinity*—inspired by political shenanigans and cultural idiosyncrasies. The playfulness, absurdity, language and truth of *The Bald Soprano* by Eugène Ionesco and *Ubu Roi* by Alfred Jarry contributed to the spirit and qualities of this satirical story.

A team of actors, technicians, designers and stage managers worked tirelessly and collectively to bring the script to life: Max Sopkin, Ashleigh Droz, Kyle McCurdy, Ryan Joseph Austin, Melanie Marshall, Arash Shahabi, Shelby Lewis, Justin P. Campbell, Ellen Jones, Redzuan Abdul Rahim, Victoria Doroski, Matt Hranek, Jillian Voss, Jaide Whitman, Thomas John Bernard, Tim Dugan, Thomas Schneider, Paul Cha and Howard Gee.

Thank you to Ellyn Gersh-Lerner, adjudicator for KCACTF (Kennedy Center American College Theatre Festival), an advocate for the play.

Special thanks to Linda Halisky, Dean of the College of Liberal Arts, California Polytechnic State University, San Luis Obispo, for her support, enabling the play to receive a wider audience.

I'm grateful to Bix Skahill who had the courage to publish the prose version.

A trio of dear friends, Andrew Campbell, Malia McDiarmid and Erma Stauffer, have been invaluable in shaping my artistic endeavors, providing encouraging words while challenging me to explore new forms of expression.

And a most special acknowledgement to Wyatt Brown, a constant, reliable partner and source of feedback. I count on Wyatt to read and edit my work, offer honest opinions and walk the tightrope between critic and cheerleader.

AL SCHNUPP is the award-winning author of the plays *My Body, Censored, Zero to Infinity, The Site, Living Stones, Antigone and Letters to Soldiers Lost, CrossRoads, The Collection, The MerryWinkle International Troupe of Vagabonds Performs a Delicious Potpourri of Fantastical Fairy Tales and Astonishing Folk Legends*, as well as an improvisational game book, *Bravo!*, and the novella, *Goods and Effects*. He also co-authored *The Stone Circle*, a full-length adult puppet show, which won an UNIMA International Citation of Excellence. He recently retired from teaching at California Polytechnic State University, San Luis Obispo, and holds a doctorate from UCLA. As a visual artist, he participates in a variety of art and craft festivals in California and has shown his work in several galleries.